A SERIES OF MURDERS

SIMON BRETT,
And His
Charles Paris Mysteries

"The most engaging new murder-solver in recent years has been Simon Brett's Charles Paris."
—**Charles Champlin, *Los Angeles Times***

■

"A highly entertaining series."
—**Marilyn Stasio, *Philadelphia Inquirer***

"Brett knows the British stage inside out, and backgrounds are unusually authentic."
—**Newgate Callendar,
*New York Times Book Review***

■

"Quite simply, the best in the business."
—***Kirkus Reviews***

■

"The modern-day resolution ties up the tale with an unexpected twist."
—***Publishers Weekly***

■

more...

A SERIES OF MURDERS

A CHARLES PARIS MYSTERY
SIMON BRETT

WARNER BOOKS

A Time Warner Company

WARNER BOOKS EDITION

This Warner Books Edition is published by arrangement with Charles Scribner's Sons, an imprint of Macmillan Publishing Company, 866 Third Avenue, New York, NY 10022.

Cover illustration by John Martinez

Warner Books, Inc.
666 Fifth Avenue
New York, N.Y. 10103

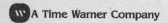 A Time Warner Company

Printed in the United States of America

First Warner Books Printing: November, 1990

10 9 8 7 6 5 4 3 2 1

To Alan and Peta
(not forgetting Petra)

CHAPTER
<u>ONE</u>

"Now listen, lads, we're dealing with a cold-blooded murderer who will stop at nothing."

Sergeant Clump stared belligerently over the counter of Little Breckington Police Station at the dozen constables facing him. "And that is why you've been gathered here from all corners of the county to see that his evil plans are foiled." He leaned forward as he warmed to his task. "Now, there's only one thing that's going to defeat a criminal of such cunning, and that is—"

"Superior cunning," a voice from the doorway coolly interrupted.

The thirteen policemen turned as one to look at the newcomer. They saw a tall figure in a dark floppy hat and cloak. A monocle graced one eye; from it a dark cord snaked down to the buttonhole of an immaculately tailored suit. A pale cravat frothed at the stranger's neck; white spats gleamed above the shine of his black shoes.

"Mr. Braid," said Sergeant Clump in a voice that combined admiration and resentment in equal parts. "I wondered when you was going to turn up. But don't you worry, sir. Everything's in hand. We shall catch this devil without needing your assistance."

"Really?" Stanislas Braid wafted across the room and came to rest in a chair by the counter. He looked up at the sergeant; his expression was quizzical, challenging, almost insolent. "Well, I suppose there has to be a first time for everything."

The sergeant's face contorted into frustration. He looked, as the police always should when faced by the coruscating brilliance of an amateur sleuth, baffled.

They held each other's gaze for a long time. Much longer, indeed, than would have been expected in the normal course of events. Then, mercifully, a new voice released them. "Okay, we've got that."

At the floor manager's words the assembled policemen on the set relaxed, broke their formal stances, and turned to chatter and giggle with each other. Charles Paris eased his finger around the neck of Sergeant Clump's jacket. Uncomfortable, those prewar high-collared uniforms. And hot under the television lights.

Russell Bentley, the actor playing Stanislas Braid, shook his head with dissatisfaction. There was clearly something in the scene he hadn't felt happy with.

The floor manager held up a finger, indicating that the cast should stay in position, while he listened to his earpiece for instructions from the gallery. He nodded as he took in his orders, no doubt already tactfully rephrasing the director's words.

One final vigorous nod. "Yes, we're okay on that. Got the scene. Extras won't be wanted again till after lunch. Russell, you've got a costume change."

At this signal, the dozen policemen broke ranks. Though they would rather have been called background artistes than extras, they weren't going to argue. Their more immediate priority was to get to the canteen before the rush. They were a docile breed, content to spend long days over endless cups of coffee waiting for their two minutes of anonymous performance.

Charles Paris looked at where his watch should be and remembered with annoyance that the one provided by Wardrobe didn't work. His own had been thought too modern for the vaguely thirties setting of the *Stanislas Braid* series. Still, Charles reckoned the West End Television bar must be open by now. Time for a quick one, surely.

Russell Bentley, however, was set to frustrate such intentions. "Oh, come on," he complained. "We can't take that scene like that."

Everyone on the set froze truculently. The star, with the instincts of long experience in television, addressed his remarks to the one camera on whose top a red light glowed, knowing that its output could be seen in the gallery. "It was terrible."

Though he was speaking to the camera, the reply from the director was relayed through the floor manager's earpiece. "Rick said it was fine, Russell."

"But it wasn't. Camera three certainly wasn't tight enough on me at the end."

"It was fine, and we are rather pushed for time," the floor manager assured him, bowdlerizing the words that burned in his earpiece.

"That's not the point," Russell Bentley objected. "Look, if the schedule's too tight, that's not my problem. All I know is that I've got a professional reputation and I'm not going to have it destroyed by slapdash direction."

The floor manager's long training in keeping a straight face could not totally suppress a wince at the gallery's reaction to that. He smothered it in a conciliatory smile. "Rick says it was really great, and we must move on."

"Just take a cutaway of my reaction," Russell Bentley bargained, knowing that his suggestion should be quicker than retaking the whole scene. The cutaway would mean recording just the one shot and slotting it in when the scene was edited.

The floor manager's smile was diluted by more vitriol in his earpiece. "Rick said it really did look fine," he paraphrased inadequately.

"No, I'm sorry. I refuse to do the costume change until we get this right." The background artistes stirred with uneasy fascination as Russell Bentley became more "difficult."

"Look, this is the first episode of the series. Already some of the filming has been pretty unsatisfactory, though perhaps it can be tidied up in editing. But you've got to understand, the performances we lay down now are the ones we're going to be stuck with for five more episodes— more, if we go to a second series. So I'm afraid no bloody schedule is going to get in the way of my playing Stanislas Braid as I think he should be played!"

To Charles this sounded a bit rich. If there was one thing Russell Bentley was known for throughout the business, it was the fact that he played every part in exactly the same way—as Russell Bentley. He had started to play Russell Bentley when he was developed as a film star by the Rank "Charm School" and had seen no reason to change the formula when his career developed into television. The idea that it took him time to home in on a new characterization was incongruous.

But at the same time Charles knew that what was going on was not really a discussion of the character of Stanislas Braid. It was a power struggle between Russell Bentley and the director, Rick Landor. The star wanted the guidelines for his treatment during the series to be established early on and was prepared to use his considerable experience in manipulation to get his own way. Rick Landor was a relatively new director, and Russell was determined to break the young man in. They'd already had a set-to on Monday, the first day of filming, and now, on Wednesday, Russell was trying to assert his authority over the studio part of the production, too.

Still, Charles thought, mustn't complain, just take anything that comes along. After all, he was working, actually contracted till the end of June for a whole television series of six programs, three months' highly paid work— When was the last time that had happened to Charles Paris?

Russell Bentley won this round of the struggle. Rick Landor, no doubt deciding that the loss of time promised by further argument was greater than the loss of time involved in taking the single shot, capitulated.

"Okay, we'll do the cutaway," the floor manager

relayed, failing to disguise his relief at the end of the skirmish.

As always, such things take longer than they should. The continuity of the characters' positions and eyelines had to be checked on the recorded tape and the background artistes regrouped exactly as they had been on the first take. Charles Paris had to be moved by millimeters back and forth along his counter. Then Russell Bentley was not happy with his expression in the first two takes of the cutaway. By the time the shot was finally in the can, it would have been quicker to retake the whole scene.

"Okay, break for coffee there," the floor manager shouted. He consulted his watch. "Back at twenty past eleven."

Oh, damn, thought Charles, it's earlier than I thought. Have to wait a while for that drink.

He grinned across to a girl standing at the edge of the set. She, too, was dressed in thirties style: a pastel summer dress, a neat little hat perched on the back of her head, hair corrugated by a perm. But the girlish costume seemed at odds with her dark, almost Italian coloring and the thick sensuality of her lips.

"Going for a coffee?" asked Charles, who hadn't had the opportunity to talk to her much during the previous week of rehearsal and two days of filming and thought he might make up for lost time.

"Maybe in a while," Sippy Stokes replied diffidently.

So Charles went off to the canteen on his own.

The scene in the W.E.T. canteen might have looked bizarre to an outsider, but the people there were used to seeing tables filled with thirties policemen and bright young things in striped blazers from the *Stanislas Braid* set, exotically crested and miniskirted dancers from a pop program in Studio B, along with the usual makeup girls in nylon tabards, PAs in designer leisurewear, shirt-sleeved cameramen, T-shirted scene shifters, and the occasional sharp executive suit.

Charles bought his subsidized cup of coffee and Eccles cake and reflected, not for the first time, on how much he always found himself eating when working in television. It's all those breaks, he thought, all those oh-so-available subsidized canteens. Even worse when doing the filming— location caterers providing lavish spreads, people who would never normally eat between meals cramming every spare moment with a bacon sandwich. He sometimes wondered whether Wardrobe had problems with long series, constantly having to let out the stars' waistbands. Though the stars were probably working so hard that they burned it all off. It was the supporting artistes who faced the real hazard of obesity, he concluded as his stomach strained against Sergeant Clump's belt.

The table he joined was, predictably enough, a theatrical one. A couple of the policeman-extras, who still thought of themselves as actors and were not yet reconciled to a lifetime of "background" work, were sitting there.

Also in uniform, though in his case a gray chauffeur's uniform, was Jimmy Sheet, who played Stanislas Braid's faithful driver, Blodd. Though Sheet was now concentrating on acting, the admiring glances of a few secretaries in the canteen reminded Charles that the young man had only recently given up his career as a pop singer.

The others at the table were Will Parton, Mort Verdon, and Tony Rees, the last two stage manager and assistant stage manager, respectively. Charles had worked with Mort on a previous W.E.T. series, *The Strutters*, and appreciated the willowy man's outrageously camp humor. Tony Rees he didn't know well, but he had a lot of time for Will Parton, the writer who had adapted most of the *Stanislas Braid* scripts from the crime novels of W. T. Wintergreen. Will had a good line in cynical repartee, which was responding well to Mort's contrasting style as Charles joined them.

"Right, tell me, who's this an impression of?" Mort demanded, suddenly erasing all expression from his face and freezing.

"A zombie?" Will hazarded.

"Close, close." Mort relaxed. "No, that was Russell Bentley looking happy."

"Ah, of course."

"And this one?" Mort recomposed his face into exactly the same anonymous pose.

This time Will caught on. "Russell Bentley looking sad!"

"Exactly, boofle," Mort agreed. "And this morning, of course, we saw Russell Bentley stamping her little foot, didn't we?"

"Missed that," said Will. "I wasn't in the studio."

With relish in the telling, Mort supplied the details of the recent conflict.

"I don't blame him," Will said at the end of the narration, "if he's having problems finding the character. I've read every one of the bloody books of W. T.

Wintergreen, and dear Stanislas Braid still seems completely cardboard to me.''

"But then dear Russell is a completely cardboard actor,'' Mort observed judiciously, "so it's actually very good casting.''

"Which is more than can be said for some of the other casting,'' Jimmy Sheet announced.

Mort cocked a quizzical eyebrow at him. "Now who *could* you mean?''

"Are you not feeling at home in the role of Blodd yet?'' asked Will.

"What?'' Jimmy Sheet was instantly on the defensive. "Don't you worry, I can manage it fine. All right, I know I done the singing for a few years, but I started out as an actor. Italia Conti School, all that.''

"That wasn't what I meant,'' Will reassured Jimmy. But Charles wondered. Will was very good at needling people in an ambiguous way; he had an infallible knack of homing in on someone's insecurities.

"All I was saying,'' Will continued soothingly, "is that the lovely W. T. Wintergreen has put almost exactly as much reality into the character of Blodd as she has into dear old Stanislas himself. I don't envy you playing the part.''

"Oh, I reckon it's all right,'' said Jimmy. "Not too hard. Way I see him, Blodd's a sort of fairly chirpy cockney type, you know, good to have around, keeps everyone cheerful. Bit of an eye for the girls, too.''

Will Parton nodded gravely. "I'm glad you see it that way. Because that's exactly how I've written the part.''

Charles caught Will's eye, and both of them had to look away to avoid giggling. Jimmy Sheet didn't realize he was being sent up. The character he had described had very little to do with the character of Blodd as written, but it was a very good portrait of how Jimmy Sheet saw himself. Just as Russell Bentley was playing Russell Bentley, so Jimmy Sheet clearly intended to play Jimmy Sheet.

"Has W. T. W. herself been around today?" asked Charles diffidently, shifting the subject.

"She was in the gallery this morning," Mort confirmed. "With her dear loopy sister."

"And they were both poking round the set first thing," added Tony Rees in his truculent Welsh voice. "Disapproving of all the props and that."

Will laughed bitterly. "How's Rick bearing up to them?"

"With difficulty."

"I can imagine. I make a solemn vow"—the writer laid his hand on his heart—"that in future I will only adapt the works of *dead* authors. I cannot stand any more of the genteel interference of people like W.T.W. and Louisa. Why can't they do what all other writers involved in television do—just take the money, do as they're told, and shut up?"

The deep cynicism of this reminded Charles of Will's unsuccessful attempts to be an original playwright and the contempt in which he held his lucrative television contracts.

"Anyway, I think there'll be tears before bedtime," said Mort Verdon piously. "Poor young Rick is not finding life easy between the demands of his aging star and his extremely aged crime writer."

"Not to mention his rather less aged starlet," Will threw in casually.

"Who do you mean?" asked Charles.

But Jimmy Sheet knew straightaway. With a smile of complicity to Will, he said, "That was what I meant about casting."

"Ah."

"Not the greatest little actress in the world, I'd say."

"As an actress, Sippy Stokes is absolute death." Then Will added mischievously, "And she hasn't even got the excuse of having been a pop star for the last five years."

" 'Ere, what do you think you're—?"

"I was joking, Jimmy. Just joking."

Jimmy Sheet subsided with a grin, but he didn't look totally reassured. Once again, Will's attack—if attack it was—had been ambiguous.

Sippy Stokes, the object of their bitchery, had been cast for the series in the role of Stanislas Braid's beloved daughter, Christina. This was another character who worked better for enthusiasts of the crime novels of W. T. Wintergreen than for Will Parton. He had had considerable difficulties in making the part even vaguely playable, though he was quite pleased with the lines he had eventually come up with. Played by an actress of real skill and energy, he reckoned they would just about work.

On the evidence of the rehearsal of the previous week and of that week's filming, Sippy Stokes was not such an actress. Even Russell Bentley, usually far too absorbed in giving his performance as Russell Bentley to notice what any of the rest of the cast did, had been heard to comment on her incompetence.

"No, some people are born actresses," Will Parton mused aloud, "some achieve actressness, but I'm afraid you could thrust everything you liked upon Sippy Stokes and you'd never make her into one."

"She speaks well of you, too," said Mort.

"Well, quite honestly," Will persisted. "I would have thought the basic minimum requirement for an actress is the ability to act."

"Don't you believe it, boofle. Lots of actresses have made very good careers from completely different 'minimum requirements.'"

"Nell Gwynne, for example," Charles suggested.

"Yes, very good example. I mean, she did all right. Now there was a girl who knew her onions."

"Or her oranges."

"Thank you, Charles—always rely on you for a cheap line, can't we? Point I'm making, boofle, is that you never hear much about what old Nellie was like *as an actress*, do you. Never read any notices . . . 'Nell Gwynne made an enchanting Ophelia . . .'"

"Or even 'I would have enjoyed the evening more without Nell Gwynne's Juliet.'"

"Yes. Mind you, Charles, I don't think any critic would be quite *that* vicious."

"Ah." Charles grimaced apologetically.

"Oh, really? Who?"

"*Surrey Advertiser.* And I'm afraid the actual line was 'I would have enjoyed the evening more without Charles Paris's Romeo.'"

"Oh, bad luck. Anyway, point I'm making, boofle, is—"

But Mort Verdon never got on to the point he was

making, for they were interrupted at that moment by the arrival of Ben Docherty, the producer, and Dilly Muirfield, the script editor, of *Stanislas Braid*. Will Parton greeted their appearance with a groan. He knew it would be him they wanted to see, and he knew it would be about more rewrites that they wanted to see him. "As someone once said," he had growled at Charles a few evenings before, "you don't write for television, you *re*write for television."

Sure enough, there were "a couple of points" on the next week's script that Ben and Dilly wanted to "just have another look at," so Will allowed himself to be dragged away, protesting that he was sure Shakespeare didn't have this trouble.

Though the coffee break had another five minutes to run, the taciturn A.S.M., Tony Rees, also reckoned it was time he was getting back to the studio, and Jimmy Sheet wanted to check some lines in his dressing room.

Mort Verdon regaled Charles with a few scurrilous stories about Ben Docherty's drinking, mostly along the lines of "My dear, he was once so pissed he contracted a whole cast for a series one afternoon, completely forgot he'd done it, and contracted a completely different lot the next morning," but then he, too, had to return to check through some props for the next scene.

That left Charles with his two policemen, the background artistes.

"This is the first episode, isn't it?" asked one of them.

Charles confirmed that that was indeed the case.

"And that police station is a regular set?"

"Oh, yes."

"And you're a running character?"

"Yes," said Charles, still having a bit of difficulty in accepting his unusual good fortune. "In every episode."

"Ah." The background artiste nodded with satisfaction. "That's good."

Charles was curious. "Why?"

"Well, you're always going to need policemen on a police-station set, aren't you?"

"Um . . ."

The background artiste winked at his companion. "And got to keep familiar faces, haven't you? Can't keep changing the personnel in a village police station, can you? I think we could be in for a series here, Bob."

They both looked so pleased at the idea that Charles hadn't the heart to disillusion them, to tell them that the whole point of Little Breckington Police Station, as created by the inimitable W. T. Wintergreen, was that it only had one policeman. Sergeant Clump was the village bobby; he did everything on his own; it was only in this one episode that he enlisted the help of police from other areas.

But there was no need to tell the two background artistes that. Charles knew too much about theatrical dreams and hopes to crush them so gratuitously.

CHAPTER
TWO

He wandered back to the studio shortly after half past eleven. Better just check what they were moving on to next. He still quite fancied a drink, but he didn't want to look desperate. Of course, there was the half bottle of Bell's back in his dressing room, but no, he should resist that. Drinking in secret always made him feel a bit like a secret drinker. Whereas having a drink in the W.E.T. bar had a more open, honest—almost virtuous—feel to it.

The rehearsal light rather than the recording light showed outside the double doors of Studio A, so Charles was not worried about slipping inside. He looked out across the five sets cunningly angled by the designer to fit into the studio space. Cameras and mobile sound booms on long cables prowled between the different locations.

Apart from the Little Breckington Police Station set,

there were the hall, sitting room, and billiard room of Breckington Manor, the stately home of Stanislas Braid (who of course had aristocratic parentage and for whom money had never been a problem).

There was also the set of the great man's study, whose bookshelves were meant to reflect his polymathic knowledge. The ornaments in the room attested to his extensive travels and the gratitude of wealthy—in many cases, regal—clients all over the world. No doubt the silver elephants expressed the thanks of some maharaja whose daughter's kidnapping Stanislas Braid had solved when the entire police force of India had been baffled. The fine decanter and glasses were no doubt the gift of a Viennese countess whose husband's murderer Stanislas Braid had unmasked when the entire police force of Austria had been baffled. The fine brass candlesticks on the mantelpiece probably bore witness to the relief of a Greek shipping magnate after Stanislas Braid had defused the bomb whose whereabouts had had the police of twelve nations baffled.

And so on, and so on. At least, thought Charles Paris, whose role as Sergeant Clump was to express the continuing bafflement of the police on a weekly basis, W.E.T. hasn't stinted on the set dressing. Everything looked very solid and real. The prop buyers must have had their work cut out to find that lot. Charles didn't think he'd ever been in a television production with so many props.

No, *Stanislas Braid* would look good. But, as so often in television, Charles worried about the difference between the look of the product and the product itself. With no discredit to Will Parton, who had worked miracles with what he had been given, the scripts did have a dated feel. Not a period feel, which, Charles suspected, was what W.E.T. was really striving for, but a dated feel. There is all the difference in the world between a loving re-creation of a past period and something that just looks old-fashioned. And though it was early on in the series to form judgments, Charles had a nasty suspicion that *Stanislas Braid* would achieve the second effect.

Nothing was actually being rehearsed when Charles came into the studio, but there was a huddle of activity over in front of the sitting-room set. He moved toward it, but as he drew closer, he realized that the activity was just another argument between Russell Bentley and his director. This time it must have been more serious, because Rick Landor had actually come down on to the studio floor and was speaking to his star without the mediation of a floor manager. Also on the scene were the thin, faded figures of W. T. Wintergreen and her sister, Louisa, no doubt contributing their own objections to the argument.

It was clearly going to be some time before anything got rehearsed, let alone recorded. And Charles wasn't even in that scene. Definitely be time for a drink. Just so long as he told someone where he was.

He moved away quietly. No need to draw attention to himself; someone might think of something he was needed for. He went around the edge of the study set into the corridor between the studio wall and the backs of the flats. The smell of canvas warmed by strong lights was achingly familiar from the backstages of a thousand theaters. Ahead of him he saw a familiar back view kneeling down at the foot of a flat. Good, someone he could tell where he was going.

"Tony."

The A.S.M. whirled around at the sound of Charles's voice. He looked flushed. "Goodness, you startled me."

"Sorry. Just wanted to say, nothing seems to be happening on the set. I'm going to nip to the bar for a quick drink, okay? Get me paged up there if I'm needed."

"Yes, fine, okay," said Tony Rees.

One of the advantages of having worked for the company a few times was that Charles knew the quickest way to the bar from almost every part of W.E.T. House. From this end of Studio A the best route was out through a dark little storage room used for props, into the scenery dock, up the stairs to the first floor, and through the Casting Department.

Cheered by the anticipation of soon having a large Bell's in his hand, Charles started on his way.

The scene that met his eyes in the murky props room was one of total chaos.

The room, probably not more than ten feet wide, was flanked with tall shelves to store props, and because of the large number required to give period flavor to *Stanislas Braid*, these were loaded. Unfortunately, no doubt because of the weight of their burden, one set of shelves must have become top-heavy and fallen forward.

The result was an amazing pile of debris, as if a bomb had gone off in a junk shop. Old cash registers lay on the floor beside elephant's foot umbrella stands; the shards of chamber pots mingled with crushed cigar boxes; billiard balls dotted their colors over a heap of smashed crockery and dented tankards.

Charles briefly contemplated telling someone about the

accident. On the other hand, a selfish instinct urged, it wasn't really his job. Someone else, whose job it might well be, would soon come through. And now the idea of an imminent drink had taken hold in his mind, Charles Paris didn't want to put it off that much longer. No, probably better all around if he just went straight to the bar.

And that is where he would have gone if he hadn't seen, protruding from the bottom of the pile of debris, something that couldn't, by the wildest stretch of the imagination, be a prop for the *Stanislas Braid* series.

It was a human hand.

A human hand that Charles had a horrible feeling he recognized.

A human hand attached to a human arm that, when Charles tried to move it from beneath the weight of the shelves, appeared to be very firmly attached to a human body.

A human hand, what's more, that was still warm. Warm but very still.

He scrabbled away at the pile of debris, and each object he moved revealed to him more of what he somehow already knew. When he saw the dress, it confirmed the message given by the hand. And the glistening blood on the dress confirmed the message of the body's stillness.

When he uncovered the head, it was, though crushed and battered, still easily recognizable as that of Sippy Stokes.

CHAPTER
<u>THREE</u>

Charles communicated the news of Sippy's death as discreetly as he could. He reckoned that since the producer is the person with overall responsibility for a production, Ben Docherty should be informed first. Fortunately, because it was still before lunch, Ben was able to take the news with appropriate sobriety. He informed the W.E.T. in-house security, who sealed off the props room and called the police.

The producer urged Charles to keep quiet about his discovery and decreed that recording should continue for as long as possible. This was avowedly to avoid panic and anxiety among the cast, but Charles knew it was also Ben fulfilling his professional role. The producer is responsible for the budgeting of a television series, and even a half day of studio time wasted is ruinously expensive. Already, so early into production, thanks to

Russell Bentley's difficulties in homing in on the character of Russell Bentley and W. T. Wintergreen's objections that Russell Bentley was nothing like the character of Stanislas Braid that she had created, the show was slipping behind schedule. The thought of that kind of time slippage escalating through a series is the stuff of which producers' nightmares are made.

The decision to continue recording, however, did not get the production much further advanced. As Charles discovered when he got back to the studio, trying to hide the state of shock he was in (and without even having had his promised large Bell's to alleviate that shock), the argument he had witnessed between star and director had arisen because Russell Bentley still wasn't happy with the way the scene in Little Breckington Police station had gone. Retaking the cutaway shot had cleared up one problem, but now he had a new cavil with something that had happened at the beginning of the recording.

Rick Landor had fought hard against the proposed retake and had enlisted Ben Docherty's support in his argument but been let down by the producer's instant capitulation. Ben Docherty, Charles was beginning to realize, was a vacillating character, and Russell Bentley was quickly getting the producer exactly where he wanted him. This did not augur well for the series. For Rick Landor to give in to the star was one thing; he was only going to be directing two of the episodes. But Ben Docherty was producer for the whole series. If he started caving in to Russell Bentley at such an early stage, it was going to be very difficult for him ever to reassert his authority.

These, however, were not Charles's problems, and he was in no condition to worry about anything except his reaction to the discovery of Sippy Stokes's body. Like most shocks, it came in little waves, suddenly weakening and unnerving him. And the words of Will Parton circled, with uncomfortable irony, around his head. "As an actress, Sippy Stokes was absolute death."

Once the production team had conceded that the police-station scene would be retaken, there was further delay, because Russell Bentley had by now changed out of the relevant costume and would have to change back again. Charles Paris waited nervously behind his counter, his mind a mess of ugly thoughts. He was hardly aware of the two policemen with whom he had had coffee jostling for position with their fellow background artistes so that they would be prominently in shot, thus staking their doomed claims to be rebooked for the rest of the series.

However much discretion Ben Docherty and the W.E.T. security men had deployed, it all went for nothing when the real police arrived. Two uniformed men and two in plain clothes marched into the studio before Russell Bentley had completed his costume change, and loudly demanded to speak to the producer. As the plainclothesmen went into a huddle with Ben Docherty, the two in uniform looked on contemptuously at the proceedings.

"Who're those two, Bob?" whispered the first background artiste with whom Charles had had coffee.

"Don't know," his friend whispered back. "Never seen them before."

"No." The first one sounded thoughtful. "I thought I knew practically everyone in the 'background' business."

"There's a new agency started up. Perhaps they're from there."

"Well, they'd better be Equity, that's all I can say."

"Yes, and why is Rick putting more in this scene, anyway? More than twelve aren't going to register in the shot, are they?"

"No. Well, just watch it when those two come in. See they don't push to the front."

"Don't worry. I'm not going to lose my position."

"Nor me." The first background artiste looked across at the two newcomers in disparagement. "Must say, I don't think they're very good."

"No. I mean, at least we look like policemen. Those two—"

"Could be postmen."

"Traffic wardens . . ."

"Anything. They look so out of place in those uniforms, don't they?"

"People just don't think when they're casting these days, do they?"

"No."

Charles was prevented from hearing further background artiste bitchery by a gesture from Ben Docherty, who beckoned him over. He obeyed and was met by the hard stare of one of the plainclothesmen. "You're the one who found the body?"

Charles nodded.

"We'll be needing to talk to you in a minute. Stay around."

"Yes."

"Just going to have a look for ourselves. Then we'll call you."

"Okay."

At that moment, Russell Bentley appeared on the scene, once again dressed in his floppy hat, cloak, and monocle. He swept up toward the group surrounding Ben Docherty.

"Here I am," he announced with a flamboyant flourish of his hat, "ready once again to prove that the plodding British policeman is no match for the gifted amateur."

"Oh, really?" said the plainclothesman in a voice as dry as a water biscuit.

The Little Breckington Police Station scene was retaken twice more, and at the end of the proceedings, when he went off once again to make his costume change, Russell Bentley had the gall to say that he thought perhaps the original take had been best, after all. The two background artistes, who lived in hope of a series booking, looked confused as they tried to remember how prominent they had been in the original take.

Charles still hadn't mentioned what lay in the props room to anyone other than Ben Docherty, but the arrival of the policemen alerted everyone on the set to the fact that something was going on. There was much whispering and curious conjecture in Studio A, but though people tried to draw him out, Charles kept his knowledge to himself.

More real policemen arrived in the studio. There was a confusion of constables as the background artistes milled and gossiped around the fringes of the set. One of the plainclothesmen bustled across to Charles. "We'll be wanting to speak to you in just a minute," he said in passing.

Charles nodded and drifted across toward the props-room door. It was dark behind the flats in this corner of the set. The outline of a uniformed policeman standing guard on the door nodded to Charles. "Hello, Sarge," it said, seeing the gleam of the stripes and unaware in the dim light of the anachronism of Sergeant Clump's uniform.

"Hello there," said Charles, seeing no reason to disillusion the constable. His actor's instinct stopped him from using his own voice. If people were going to think he was a policeman, then it was a point of honor for him to sound like a policeman. He automatically homed in on the unimpressed voice he had used as the inspector arriving in Act Three of any number of dire stage thrillers, including the one he had once played in at Colchester, whose title he had mercifully forgotten, though its review from the local paper was burned ineradicably into his memory: "I have been more thrilled by an attack of shingles than I was at any point during last night's performance."

At that moment, the props-room door opened, and a harassed-looking face peered out. "Could you give me a hand?" it appealed.

"Sorry, Doctor. Got to stay on guard," said the constable.

"What about you, Sergeant?"

"Oh, all right," said Charles Paris equably, and followed the doctor to the scene of the crime.

"Just need some help moving the shelves out of the way."

Amid the debris, the heavy shelves still pinioned the late Sippy Stokes to the ground. Charles tried not to look at the crumpled body, but even if he'd closed his eyes, he knew its disturbing imprint would still be on his mind.

"Should we be moving anything, though?" he asked, mindful of the minimal knowledge he had of scene-of-the-crime procedure.

"It's all right. The photographers have been," said the doctor.

They took one side each and heaved the wooden frame back up into position with difficulty.

"God, no one would stand much chance with this lot landing on top of them, would they?"

"No," the doctor agreed grimly. "Mind you, I don't think it was the shelves that did the damage."

"What, you mean she was dead before they fell?" In his excitement Charles used his own voice, but fortunately the doctor did not seem to notice the lapse.

"Seconds before, maybe," he replied. "It looks as if it was a blow to the back of the head that killed her. The weight of the shelves just made sure."

"So . . . you reckon someone hit her?" the sergeant asked, safely back in his sergeant's voice.

The doctor gave Charles a sardonic look. "I wouldn't say that, no. Sorry to puncture your fantasies of a nice juicy murder, Sergeant. No, I think it's more likely that some *thing* hit her."

"What kind of thing?"

The doctor gave a shrug that encompassed all the confusion of props that lay around. "Take your pick. A lot of these items would have been heavy enough. Look, there's blood on the corner of that cash register . . . and on that fire screen . . . and on those kitchen scales. . . . Just a matter of finding the piece whose outline matches the dent in the poor kid's head.''

''So what you're saying is that you reckon something fell off the shelves before the shelves themselves fell down?''

''As I said, seconds before. No, I should think the shelves were loaded so as to be top-heavy. They started to topple. . . . As they did so, various items slipped off . . . and it was one of those items that hit her on the head a split second before she got the full weight of the shelves on her.''

''But what would have made the shelves fall down?''

This prompted another shrug from the doctor. ''Who can say? Maybe they were just badly stacked. Maybe the girl was fingering something, trying to pull something out. . . . I don't know. All I do know is that West End Television is going to face a very big claim for compensation.''

''And you really don't think there's any suspicion of foul play?''

''Come on, Sergeant. Accidents happen. I don't know, I haven't done a detailed examination yet, but I'd have thought foul play was extremely unlikely.''

''Oh,'' said Charles, and the disappointment must have showed in his voice, because the doctor went on: ''For heaven's sake, man, stop being so ridiculous. You sound as if you wish there *was* a murder. You don't sound like a professional policeman at all.''

''Good heavens. Don't I?'' asked Sergeant Clump of the Little Breckington Police Station.

CHAPTER
<u>FOUR</u>

When, on the dot of six, the plugs were pulled in Studio A, everyone felt that it had been a long day. During the lunch break, the news of Sippy Stokes's death had spread throughout the *Stanislas Braid* production team, then throughout W.E.T. House, and finally, through the medium of the press and radio, to the outside world.

Ben Docherty, having had his customary alcoholic top-up at lunchtime, insisted belligerently on continuing recording through the afternoon, though it might have been more appropriate to cancel out of respect for the dead. Or respect for the living, come to that. Everyone on the set was upset by the fact of a death in the studio, though some seemed to be taking it worse than others. Rick Landor, in particular, looked shattered when he heard the news, and though he struggled gamely through the afternoon's recording, he went through the motions like an automaton.

It wasn't an easy afternoon's recording, anyway. They kept starting to rehearse scenes, only to grind to a halt when someone realized that Stanislas Braid's daughter, Christina, should have made an appearance in them. And Russell Bentley kept averring that there was no point in recording any more, anyway, because everything they'd already done would have to be scrapped when Sippy's part was recast. Charles couldn't help noticing that the star made these pronouncements with considerable relish. For Russell Bentley, Sippy Stokes's death was unadulterated good news.

In fact, it was striking how, throughout all the ranks of the production team, though everyone was suffering from shock, no one showed much sign of grief or regret. In her brief time working on *Stanislas Braid*, Sippy Stokes had not made many friends.

Charles Paris's name would never appear in *The Guinness Book of Records*, but that was only because there is no section in that work for the event called "Getting out of Costume and into the Nearest Bar." At the end of that studio day, however, he performed another Personal Best and was draped over a large Bell's before most of his fellow artistes had even made it to their dressing rooms.

Of course, he couldn't expect to compete with the production crew, who did not have the handicap of costumes and were halfway down their first pints of lager before he arrived in the W.E.T. bar.

Nor could he compete with a writer. Will Parton had

already downed his first glass of dry white and willingly accepted Charles's offer of a refill.

"So," said Will, raising his glass, "farewell, then, Sippy Stokes."

"Farewell indeed," Charles responded, shuddering slightly as the image of her body once again flashed up on the screen of his mind.

"One more unwanted person vanished into the Great Void. Prompting once again the Universal Question: What does it all mean?"

"Hmm."

"I'll tell you what it means, Charles. It means what it always means in television—more bloody rewrites!"

"Oh, but surely they won't need to change the scripts?"

"They *always* need to change the scripts—first rule of television. At least they don't always *need* to change the scripts, but they always *insist* on changing the scripts. Producers and script editors would feel they were failing in their God-given mission if they accepted a script in its original form. I tell you, if I delivered *Hamlet* to this lot, they'd come back to me with a great pile of notes. 'Wouldn't it be better if he was a bit more decisive? And there aren't really many laughs, are there? And couldn't you combine the parts of Rosencrantz and Guildernstern? Seems rather a waste to have two of them, doesn't it, because they both serve the same function? And could we cut the scene in the graveyard? Well, you know how expensive film is, and it doesn't really seem to *add* much. And as for that ending—well, talk about downbeat . . . Can't you liven it up a bit?' "

Charles chuckled. "I take your point. Was that the sort of meeting you had this morning?" Will looked at him, uncomprehending. "This morning, when Ben and Dilly dragged you out of the canteen?"

"Oh, then. No, actually that one didn't materialize. Soon as we got outside the canteen, Ben, with typical resolution, remembered there was something else he should be doing. But don't worry, the meeting is only postponed. More rewrites will still be wanted."

"I still don't see why you'll have to rewrite just because someone new's taking over the part of Christina."

"I'm sure I will have to, though. The new person they get will be totally different from Sippy, that I can guarantee."

"Why?"

"Well, this time I should think they'd get an actress."

"God, I set that up for you perfectly, didn't I?"

"Yes, Charles. Thank you very much—feed lines always appreciated."

Charles grinned. But he felt uncomfortable. He had some atavistic inhibition about speaking ill of the dead. Though his opinion of Sippy Stokes's acting abilities hadn't changed from that morning, it seemed somehow wrong to be making such comments now.

"Anyway," Will went on moodily, "even if they don't want the later scripts totally rewritten—which they almost definitely will—I've still got a lot to do on the first one, particularly now."

"What, the one we've been doing today?"

"Yes. 'The Brass Candlestick Murder.' " The writer put a world of contempt into his enunciation of W. T. Wintergreen's title.

"But surely we'll just scrap everything that Sippy recorded and redo those scenes with a new actress?"

"Don't you believe it. Oh, no, if Ben Docherty can see

a way of saving a few bob, then who cares how much extra work the mere writer has to do?''

"You mean he's intending to use the scenes with Sippy in them?''

"Yes. Not a business famous for its sentimentality, television. No, dear warmhearted Ben will salvage every last inch of tape he can. Anything rather than retaking the lot. So my latest directive this afternoon is to assemble a new jigsaw from the scenes we've already recorded and find some 'really plausible explanation'—I quote Dilly Muirfield's words—for the fact that Stanislas Braid's adored and irreproachable daughter, Christina, suddenly vanishes out of the second half of the story.''

"But that'll cock up the continuity into the next episode, surely? I mean, you can't have a completely different actress suddenly appearing as the same character.''

"Don't worry, the superbrains of the *Stanislas Braid* production team have come up with a way round that. In episode two, 'The Italian Stiletto Murder,' because Christina is still away, Stanislas Braid's *other* daughter, Elvira, suddenly returns from her finishing school in Switzerland.''

"That's ridiculous.''

"Not really. Not by the standards of the medium. Remember, Charles, we are working in television.''

"But what would W. T. Wintergreen say to her precious hero suddenly developing another daughter?''

"She has not as yet been consulted on this point. And when she is, scream and kick though she may—and scream and kick though her loopy sister Louisa may— W.E.T. will have their way with them. Stanislas Braid will sprout a second daughter.''

"Writers must have more control of what happens to their books than that."

"Depends what it says in the contract. And knowing W.E.T.'s Contracts Department, I should think they've sewn up the Stanislas Braid property in every way, right down to the merchandising of Stanislas Braid 'His 'n' Her' Bath Mats."

Charles shook his head in what he would have liked to be disbelief. But it wasn't—oh no, he found Will's words all too believable.

"Charles, in television and film the concept of writers having 'control' just does not exist. Never forget the old Hollywood story of the starlet who was so dumb she slept with the writer."

Charles laughed and accepted Will's offer of another drink. He felt like quite a few drinks that evening. He wanted to go to bed with a mind anesthetized to images of crushed and crumpled bodies.

After a long swallow of Bell's, he asked, "And is that really for real? The business about Elvira? They really want you to do it?"

"Cross my heart and hope to end up writing one-liners for David Frost. Yes, it really is true."

"But how on earth can you do it?"

"I'm a television writer," Will asserted with a deep cynicism. "They pay me, I do it."

"Well, I don't envy you that task."

"Introducing Elvira in ep. two?"

"Yes."

"Oh, don't worry about that. I've already done it."

"Done it? But Sippy only died this morning. You couldn't have had time."

"I may not be the greatest writer on earth," said Will Parton, affecting an American Drawl, "but I sure is the quickest." Then, in response to Charles's continuing expression of puzzlement, he went on: "No, actually, I did those rewrites a few days back."

"But what . . . ? Why?" Charles was at a loss. "I don't understand."

"Then I will explain it to you. I was sworn to secrecy over this, but quite honestly, now that Sippy's dead, I don't see that any harm can be done by telling you. The fact is, as we have all observed, to call Sippy Stokes an actress was an offense under the Trades Description Act."

Once again Charles winced inwardly at this attack on the dead girl.

"Well, even Ben Docherty, through his postmeridian alcoholic haze, couldn't help noticing that she had about as much talent as a bar of soap. In fact, when he saw the rushes of the first few days' filming, he knew a monumental blunder had been made. It was then that he made the decision she would have to be replaced, so Dilly Muirfield summoned me to a meeting, which witnessed the birth of Elvira and her wonderful finishing school."

"But just a minute—if Sippy was that bad, why didn't Ben just sack her and recast for the first episode?"

"What, and waste three days' filming? Anyway, all the rest of the cast were contracted. It'd be an expensive write-off. And then they'd have to find dates to make another episode, and Russell Bentley's availability gets sticky after the end of this contract."

"Ah . . . So did Sippy know she was about to be dumped?"

"Oh, no. Ben's thinking was that if she knew, there was a danger she might think, Stuff this lot, and not turn up for the remaining studio days."

"No professional actress would do that. She might be seething with fury, but she'd still turn up."

"Well, that was Ben Docherty's estimate of the situation."

"So when was she going to be told?"

"Ah, this was to be the masterpiece of television diplomacy. At the end of the final studio day on this episode."

"The day after tomorrow?"

"Right. At the end of the day, when Sippy fell, utterly knackered, into her dressing room, she would be confronted by the show's casting director."

"Ben not even doing his own dirty work?"

"Good heavens, no. Anyway, the casting director would then tell the poor kid that in spite of the fact that she'd been contracted for all six episodes, she was being paid off then and there."

"Quite a substantial payoff. She'd get everything she'd been contracted for, wouldn't she?"

"Yes, it'd be a decent lump sum. Still peanuts, though, from Ben's point of view, compared with writing off the whole episode."

"Yes," Charles mused aloud. Then a new thought struck him. "But lots of people round the production must've known. I mean, the read-through for the next episode's on Monday. They must have cast the part of Elvira by now."

"Oh, yes. They have."

"So that poor kid would have been busting a gut,

trying to act for three whole days, without knowing that she'd already been written off?''

"That would have been the situation, yes. Oh, indeedy, if it's humanity you're after, why not join the wacky world of television?"

"Shit. Well, at least she was spared the interview with the casting director."

"Yes, I should think the casting director's feeling pretty relieved, too."

"Hmm. And you're sure she didn't have an inkling of what was going on?"

"Positive."

"What about Rick? Did he know?"

"I'm fairly sure he didn't, either."

"But he must have got a copy of the new script for episode two, mustn't he?"

"No. Different director for that one. Remember, Rick's only directing alternate episodes so that he can catch up on postproduction."

"Yes, of course." Charles was silent for a moment before saying thoughtfully, "The one question all this does raise is how on earth Sippy was ever given the part in the first place."

"Ah," said Will Parton. "Now that's something I think Rick Landor *might* know."

Her voice was guarded when she answered the phone; even more guarded when she heard who was speaking.

"Charles, how are you?"

"Oh, well, you know, Frances, not so bad."

"Meaning quite bad, from your tone of voice."

"Well . . . Perhaps a bit shaken."

"And perhaps a bit drunk?"

"Perhaps a bit."

"So what's shaken you? Has something devastatingly unlikely happened . . . like your getting a job, for example?"

"I have got a job, actually. Surely I told you?"

"Charles, it's over three months since you last rang me. On that occasion, too, you chose to make your call just before midnight . . . presumably on your arrival back at Hereford Road from some bar that closed at eleven."

"I'm sorry, Frances. I didn't realize it was that late."

"Well, it is. And the last words you said to me at the end of our previous conversation three months ago were 'I'll call you before the weekend.' "

"Oh, were they?"

But Frances couldn't stay peevish for long; it wasn't in her nature. "What is it that's shaken you?" she asked in a gentler tone.

"Oh, it's—I don't know. Somebody died."

"Somebody you were close to?"

Was he being hypersensitive to hear a hint of jealousy in her voice? Though they hadn't lived together regularly for many years, Charles liked to feel that his wife still cared for him.

"No, not anyone I was close to," he replied.

"This isn't another of your murder investigations, is it, Charles?"

"No, no. At least I'm fairly sure it isn't."

"Oh, so you rang up just before midnight to tell me that someone you weren't particularly close to has died?"

"Well, yes, but . . . I wanted to hear your voice."

"This is my voice. This is what it sounds like. I think you'll find it hasn't changed a great deal in three months."

"And I want to see you." Suddenly he did, desperately. "I really want to see you, Frances."

"Ah, do you?"

"You want to see me, don't you?"

The pause that greeted this question was longer than he would have wished.

"You know, Charles," said Frances finally, "in many ways my life is much more restful when I *don't* see you."

"Yes, but then who wants their life to be restful?" he joked.

"At midnight, Charles, let me tell you, restfulness is pretty high on my list of priorities."

"I know. I'm sorry. It's unforgivably late. But look, let's make a plan to meet."

"I don't feel up to making plans now, thank you, Charles."

"But when might you feel up to making plans?"

"When you're sober," said Frances, and put the phone down.

CHAPTER
<u>FIVE</u>

Charles had drunk more heavily than someone in work should have done. The trouble was that throughout his theatrical career work had been such an intermittent visitor and stayed for such short times that his regular habits were those of someone out of work rather than those of an employed person. And his usual method of dealing with a skinful the night before—a gradual rising punctuated by black coffee, aspirins, and retreats back to bed until the blessed relief of a pint around eleven-thirty—was unsuitable for someone who had a nine o'clock makeup call at W.E.T. House.

He did make it, but his head pounded, his skin felt very tight, as though he had had face-lifts all over his body, and the makeup girl's job was made more difficult by the fact that he had the shakes. He quipped that she might do better not to try rubbing the makeup into his face but simply to hold the sponge out and let him tremble against it. She didn't appear to be amused by the idea.

No one seemed to know what the day's studio schedule would be. Normally reliable sources of all information, like Mort Verdon and the floor manager, could offer no help. Everything was disorganized. The sudden departure of Sippy Stokes had made a bigger hole in the production than anyone had realized the previous day.

Eventually some sort of running order was concocted. Basically they were going to pick up any scenes they could that didn't involve Christina Braid. Will Parton—also somewhat the worse for wear—was on hand for necessary script carpentry, sawing the beginnings and ends off scenes and making the stumps look as tidy as possible.

But there was a kind of lethargy about everything. Russell Bentley walked through his scenes in a muted way, already determined that the whole episode should be remade from the start. And the absence of W. T. Wintergreen and her sister added to the sense that the proceedings weren't really important.

The producer and director did their best. Ben Docherty, full of the positive aggression that characterized all of his actions before lunchtime, urged the cast on to greater efforts. And Rick Landor, still looking ghastly, did all the right things with a kind of nerveless deliberation. Deep down, though, both of them seemed to have lost the will to continue.

Charles was only involved in a couple of scenes on the set of Stanislas Braid's study. Both followed the usual pattern of their encounters, in which the gifted amateur ran circles around the ponderous professional. The second scene seemed only to have been inserted in the script to plant the pair of candlesticks on Stanislas Braid's mantelpiece, the candlesticks that he was to use so brilliantly to reenact the murderer's crime at the episode's denouement. The denouement itself they could not record. The character of Christina was so integral to that scene that it would require from Will not a quick bit of carpentry but a major act of cabinetmaking.

Charles went listlessly through the motions, vowing throughout the morning that he would never touch another drop of alcohol and, after a couple of drinks at lunchtime, thinking throughout the afternoon that his morning's vows had been perhaps a little rash. He dutifully did all that he was instructed to do, lifting and putting down the candlesticks endlessly while Rick Landor tried to frame his shots against the bored barracking of Russell Bentley.

By five o'clock they had run out of scenes that they could even pretend were worth doing, and Will made it clear in no uncertain terms that there was no chance of his having done the monumental rewriting required by the following morning. So Ben Docherty, whose customary early-afternoon belligerence had by now given way to a sleepy acquiescence, was forced to recognize the inevitable. The following day's studio would have to be scrapped. Reluctantly, knowing the effect it would have on his budget, he told the assembled company that they would not be called for Friday and instructed Mort Verdon to ring round the remainder of the cast and give them the news.

Charles Paris changed more slowly this time. He was not after a Personal Best now, merely trying to eke out the time until the bar opened at half past five. His morning headache had returned; he was determined not to drink as much that evening. But then Charles Paris's life was a long catalog of such determinations.

Changing out of costume and punctiliously scouring the last speck of makeup off his face only lasted him till twenty past five, so he took an atypically long route to the bar. He went through the Studio A control gallery, vaguely looking for Rick Landor, but the only person he found there was Mort Verdon, pressing down the buttons of the telephone after another of his calls to the cast.

"Rick around, Mort?"

"No, boofle. Editing. Suite three. He was booked from six, but he managed to move it since we broke early."

"Hmm. He seemed quite cut up about Sippy dying," Charles hazarded.

"Yes, well, he would be. I think he and Miss Wooden might have been rather close."

"How close?"

"Close enough to get splinters," said Mort Verdon archly. "And close enough for Rick to get the teeniest bit tetchy when Jimmy Sheet started switching on the charm."

"When did that happen? I didn't notice anything."

"No, takes a trained eye."

"What happened? What did your trained eye see?"

"Well, didn't really see anything while we were in rehearsal or filming. But I happened to see them together in Stringfellow's on Tuesday night."

"Stringfellow's? I didn't know that was your scene, Mort."

"Lot of things you don't know about me, Charles Paris." The stage manager winked at him slyly. "Mind you, *any*time you want to find out more . . . you have only to ask."

* * *

Charles had one large Bell's in the bar before setting off to find Rick. As he approached the editing suites, he was once again struck by the unequal distribution of work load in television. Every production was surrounded by an enormous team of people, but the only ones who really had to work hard were the designer, the director, and the director's production assistant. And of those the director had to work hardest. It was typical that after a long day in the studio Rick Landor would be faced by an evening's videotape editing. Or an evening's film editing. Or an evening preparing a camera script. It was a stressful job.

And a job that could be made even more stressful if one had a girlfriend who had died.

Through the glass panel of the door of suite 3, Charles could see Rick lounging back in a chair. The director appeared to be on his own, and with no audience to hold himself together for, he had allowed his face to show the strains of the last few days. He looked up at the discreet tap on the door and composed his expression into something more purposeful and energetic.

He gestured Charles to enter. "What can I do for you?" he asked.

Charles hadn't really planned what the excuse for his visit would be but homed in on something safe. "Just wondered if you might be down for a drink in the bar later?"

It wasn't that strange a suggestion. The director and actor had met for the occasional quick drink over the last week. And though Charles's coming all the way to the

editing suite to make his invitation might have seemed
unusual, Rick did not appear to notice any incongruity.

"I doubt it, actually, Charles. I'm pretty bushed. And
I'm booked in here till nine—well, half past eight, 'cause
we started early—but I think after that I'll head straight
back home. Thanks for the idea, though."

"Oh, well, plenty of other opportunities."

"Sure."

Charles looked around the suite. Videotape is not
edited like film. The tape is not actually cut; different
takes are joined together by a process of dubbing from
one machine to another. Digital displays show the position of the various tapes. At that moment, the large
machines, with their giant spools, stood idle. On the
monitor in front of Rick, Stanislas Braid was frozen in
his study, caught in mid-gesture.

Answering Charles's unspoken question, the director
said, "P.A.'s getting coffee, and the editor's gone to get
another tape. Library didn't send up all we needed.
Another cock-up."

Charles nodded. "Bit of a chapter of cock-ups the last
few days have been," he said, trying to open out the
conversation.

"You can say that again."

"I didn't know Sippy very well."

"No. I did."

There was no ambiguity in Rick's tone. He made no
attempt to hide the relationship. In fact, he seemed more
than ready to expand on it. "My marriage broke up three
years ago."

Of course, Charles remembered, a broken marriage
was virtually an essential qualification for a young direc-

tor in television. Mind you, he reminded himself with a little shiver at the recollection of Frances's coldness on the telephone, I'm a fine one to criticize.

"Sippy was the first girl I'd got even vaguely involved with since. Not that it was that serious, but . . ."

"I'm sorry. It must have been hell for you the last couple of days."

"Not great, but . . . the show must go on," said Rick grimly. "Can't think about that sort of thing too much when you're working. And I seem to be working every hour God sends at the moment."

"Yes, I was just thinking that as I came along here."

"Still, can't complain. At least the work's there," said the director brusquely. "And I do love television."

"Really?" said Charles, for whom the only really attractive thing about television was the money.

"Yes, I love it. Even though it broke up my marriage— Well, I suppose it wasn't all television's fault. The fact that my wife was a promiscuous little bitch might have had something to do with it, too. . . . And now television has broken up another relationship for me."

"You blame television for Sippy's death?" asked Charles, eager to pounce on any stray clue that might be about.

"No, not really. I just mean that she died in a television studio, that's all."

There seemed something evasive about the way Rick spoke, as if he had started to say something else and then decided to backtrack.

"You heard that I actually found her body, did you?"

"Yes. Must've been nasty."

"Was." There was a silence. "I had to talk to the police."

"Me, too."

"Didn't elicit much from them about what they thought had happened."

"Nor did I," said Rick unhelpfully.

Charles looked at the picture on the monitor screen. Something in it caught his attention. Masking his excitement in casualness, he asked, "When did you record that scene?"

"That? Oh, immediately after the break yesterday morning. It's hardly a scene, really. It's just one of those moments of Russell sitting in his study with a cigar and looking thoughtful."

"The Great Mind at work. Stanislas Braid's Mighty Intellect solves another case."

"That's it. There'll be a good few of those shots through the series."

"Hard to tell how it's going at this stage," Charles prompted diffidently.

Rick Landor looked up at him with a cynical smile. "Well, I don't think it's going to be Miss Marple."

"What do you mean?"

"That's W.E.T.'s idea. Look at the sales round the world of the BBC's Miss Marple series—that's the bandwagon they're trying to hitch on to. They think, Let's get something of the same kind . . . detective stories . . . lots of period detail. . . . We'll clean up. Hmm, well, I think they may have miscalculated."

"Why?"

"For a start, W. T. Wintergreen is no Agatha Christie."

"And Russell Bentley is no Joan Hickson."

"No. And then again, the way they're making it is all wrong. W.E.T.'s trying to do it on the cheap, as usual. I mean, that half-on-film and half-in-studio stuff just looks so old-fashioned nowadays. The international market wants series that're all on film."

"And you'd much rather be directing something that's all on film?"

"Need you ask?"

No, Charles needn't have, really. All television directors think they're film directors manqué. And most of them nurse secret fantasies of one day single-handedly reviving the British feature-film industry.

"About Sippy..." Charles began again.

"Hmm?" Rick responded wearily.

"Your relationship was still happening... you know, when she died?"

The director's eyes narrowed. For the first time he showed signs of resenting Charles's probing. "What makes you ask that?"

"I don't know. You just didn't seem to take much notice of each other round the studio."

"There is such a thing as professionalism, Charles."

"Yes, yes, of course. I know." There is also such a thing, he reflected, as not wishing to draw attention to the operations of the casting couch. Particularly if the person cast did not show such exceptional abilities on a television set as she presumably did on the couch.

"No," he went on, taking a calculated risk. "I mean, if I'd been asked to say who—if anyone—in the company Sippy was tied up with, I'd probably have plumped for Jimmy Sheet."

That one hit home. Rick Landor's eyes blazed. "Well, you would have been wrong, then, wouldn't you, Charles?"

But the vehemence of the denial meant that the matter was at least worthy of further investigation.

Not at that moment, though. The editor had just returned with the right tape, and at the same time Rick's P.A. appeared with a tray of coffee and packets of biscuits. Charles made his good-byes.

He may not have got much information out of Rick Landor, but the visit to the editing suite had filled him with a bubble of excitement. Something he had seen there had brought bursting to the surface an idea that he had vigorously suppressed since his discovery of Sippy's body.

The frozen picture of Stanislas Braid's study on the editing monitor had differed in one particular from the set on which Charles had worked that afternoon. Differed indeed from the set that he had seen when he returned from his coffee break the previous morning.

On the later occasions there had been two candlesticks on Stanislas Braid's mantelpiece. In the scene that had been recorded about the time of Sippy Stokes's death, only one candlestick was in evidence.

Where was the other one?

Was it fanciful to imagine that the base of a candlestick might fit the dent in the young actress's head?

Or fanciful to imagine that Sippy Stokes had been murdered?

CHAPTER
<u>SIX</u>

It was a novel experience for Charles to ring his agent when he was working. Usually, such calls were made during those long sags in his career when it looked as if nobody would ever employ Charles Paris again in the history of the universe. At such times, though ringing his agent didn't actually help—Maurice Skellern was so incompetent that he never knew of any jobs coming up—it did at least spread the misery.

But for that Friday morning's call the circumstances were totally different. Charles was at the beginning of a three-month contract for W.E.T. For once in his life he had a guaranteed income; he could see some way ahead financially—not very far ahead, it was true, but three months further ahead than he usually could. So it was almost with an air of condescension that he dialed his agent's number.

"Maurice Skellern Artistes," the voice at the other end of the line grudgingly conceded.

"Maurice, it's Charles."

"Oh, Charles, I nearly rang you yesterday."

"Really?" For Maurice to have rung him would have been almost unprecedented.

"Had a couple of availability checks."

"On me?" That, too, was an event of sufficient rarity to be included in one of Arthur C. Clarke's collections of astounding phenomena.

"Yes, it was some feature-film company and . . . oh, er, yes, the National Theatre."

"What? Why on earth didn't you contact me?"

"Well, you're not available, are you, Charles? You're tied up with W.E.T. for the next three months."

"Yes, but . . ." It was true, though. Wasn't that typical of his life, Charles thought bitterly. For nearly two years his phone had been so silent he had kept considering getting British Telecom to check whether it was still working; for two years the producers, directors, and casting directors of every theater, film, and television company in the world had been clinically immune to the magnetism of his talent; and then suddenly, once he was working, the interest started flooding in.

Or did it? He had no proof that the calls had actually happened. And inventing them was an excellent way for Maurice to make it look as if he were being a punctilious agent. Though Charles was not basically a suspicious person, he took much of what his agent told him with a cautionary pinch of salt.

"Did they really call, Maurice?"

"Who?" came the innocent reply.

"These people from the film company and the National."

"Charles, would I lie to you?"

Yes, of course you would, you old bastard. And often have. But he didn't voice the thought. What was the point?

Maurice moved hastily on, not giving his client time for second thoughts about answering his question. "Nasty business you had in the studio the other day."

"What?"

"That actress. Slippy. . . ?"

"Sippy. Mind you, that's no less silly than Slippy. Yes, she had chosen to call herself Sippy Stokes. At least I assume she had chosen it. No one's actually christened 'Sippy,' are they?"

"Wouldn't have thought so. At least she'd have been safe with Equity. No likelihood of a clash with someone else of the same name."

"True."

"Nasty business, though. Getting crushed by all those props falling on top of her."

"Maurice, how is it that you know all this?"

"Like to keep my ear to the ground."

"Yes, but how is it that you keep your ear to the ground to pick up all the gossip but never know who's doing any casting or where there are any jobs going?"

"Ah, now, come on, Charles, be fair. Who was it who tickled up the interest from this feature-film company and the National Theatre?"

It was wonderful, Charles reflected, how these two— probably fictitious—calls out of the blue to check availability had now metamorphosed into opportunities that Maurice had painstakingly engineered on his client's behalf. But once again it wasn't worth pointing out the anomaly.

"Anyway," his agent went on, "be a big compensation bill for W.E.T."

This seemed to be a universal first reaction to the news of Sippy Stokes's death.

"Yes, I guess so. Incidentally, since you seem to know everything about it," Charles went on with heavy but wasted irony, "you haven't heard any suggestions that the death was not an accident, have you?"

"What, murder or something like that, you mean?"

"Well, it's a thought. She wasn't the most popular person round the production."

"No, haven't heard anything like that. Isn't the buzz I'm getting from my sources, anyway."

Not for the first time in their relationship, Charles wondered who on earth Maurice's "sources" might be. Whoever they were, they were pretty good. For relaying gossip, that is. Not for the business of finding out where the jobs were. In that they were as hopeless as Maurice Skellern himself.

"Mind you," the agent continued, "I gather the police are still investigating, so maybe something'll come out at the inquest."

"Well, if you do hear anything, Maurice..."

"I'll let you know. And anytime, anything you want found out, so long as it's in 'the business,' you know you have only to ask."

"Sure."

"But," said Maurice, moving on with enthusiasm, "have you heard who's taking over Sippy Stokes's part?"

There was a particular note of glee that always came

into his voice when he was imparting information he felt confident his audience didn't know, and it was there as he asked this question.

"No. No, I knew they'd recast, but I haven't heard who it's going to be."

"Name 'Joanne Rhymer' mean anything to you?"

"The 'Rhymer' bit does, obviously. Any relation to Gwen Rhymer?"

"Daughter."

"Ah." The name brought back not wholly unpleasant memories for Charles. "I wonder if she shares her mother's well-known proclivities?"

"Which proclivities?"

"I was only thinking of the promiscuity, actually. I mean, in the old days Gwen Rhymer used to be called the Blue Nun."

"Blue Nun?"

"Yes, like the wine."

"Eh?" Maurice was being more than usually obtuse.

"Blue Nun is recommended as the ideal accompaniment to all meals," Charles spelled out, "and Gwen Rhymer used to be called the Blue Nun because she . . . went with everything."

"Ah, with you. Nice one, Charles, nice."

"So her daughter's getting the part . . . hmm. Big advantage that can be for a young actress, having a parent in the business."

"Yes, well, if you think of the number of producers who probably still fancy getting inside the lovely Gwen's pants, the daughter could pick up quite a few favors, I'd imagine."

"And of course if she does carry on the family tradition, she could pick up a good few in her own right. Oh, well, I will look forward to meeting her on Monday. That's when we've got the read-through for ep. two, 'The Italian Stiletto Murder.' ''

"Still having read-throughs, are you?"

"What do you mean?"

"Well, most series like this, once you get up and running, they dispense with the read-through. Go straight into rehearsal."

"I think to call the *Stanislas Braid* series 'up and running' would be a gross distortion of the truth, Maurice. Apart from the problems raised by the recasting, Russell Bentley's making very heavy weather of the whole thing. He's not going to give up the read-throughs in a hurry. They give him his first opportunity to cut new directors down to size."

"Dear, oh, dear," said Maurice with fond nostalgia. "Russell Bentley. He's been around forever. I remember all those dreadful movies in the fifties—*The Hawk's Prey*, was that one of them? They were all stinkers, anyway, that's all I remember. Ah, well, there's always been a strong spirit of forgiveness in the British public." He chuckled. "Anyway, have fun, Charles. Keep smiling."

"Incidentally, Maurice, I'm intrigued. How is it you manage to know more about the production I'm working on than I do myself?"

"My job, isn't it? Someone's got to have their finger on the pulse of this business, haven't they? I mean, where do you think you'd be if you hadn't got me looking after your interests?"

The possible answers to this question were so varied

and the options they offered so attractive that Charles didn't bother to say anything.

Charles put down the receiver of the pay phone on the landing and went slowly back to his room. He filled the kettle and switched it on for coffee, then moved a couple of shirts spread out over his armchair in lieu of ironing and sat down.

He looked around the bed-sitter and saw it as a stranger might. Tatty, tacky, and untidy. The bed lumpy under its crumpled yellow candlewick. The furniture, which had been painted gray so long ago that it might even have been at a time when gray was trendy. The discolored, dead gas fire. The dusty plastic curtain that hid the sink and gas ring, and beside it, as if to mock his infirmity of purpose, the equally dusty but more attractive curtain he had bought some months previously to replace it.

But that sort of activity required so much effort. Well, perhaps not effort. After all, it was simply a matter of transferring the hooks from the old curtain to the new one and hanging it up. No, the problem was more one of will. He had to want to do it, had to want to make his environment attractive, to turn the anonymous room into a home.

It was something he had never been good at. Frances had been good, very good. She turned everywhere they lived into a home, and while they were living together, he had liked the warmth of that feeling. But after he had walked out on the marriage in pursuit of some unattainable concept of freedom, he had reverted to type. Reverted to the sense that everything was temporary, that he was just camping until he sorted his life out. But his life remained resolutely unsorted-out; his bed-sitter, resolutely unimproved and anonymous.

For a moment, as he looked around the room, he contemplated moving. Why not? Buy somewhere, put a foot back on the bottom rung of the property ladder he had formerly climbed with Frances. After all, at the moment he could afford it. W.E.T.'s fees were very generous. And, in spite of Rick Landor's gloomy prognostications for its success, there had been talk of a second series of *Stanislas Braid*. According to Will Parton, there were enough W. T. Wintergreen titles to do at least six more. And then they could move on to new story lines, "opening the writing out," as Dilly Muirfield put it (or "wheeling in the massed hacks," as Will put it).

Yes, this one could run and run. And having his face seen in the country's living rooms on a weekly basis might bring Charles Paris the actor back into fashion. (Well, *into* fashion—he had to admit he'd never really been there before.) Yes, it might all be all right. He probably could risk the commitment of buying somewhere.

But even as he had the thought, he knew he'd never do it. It wasn't really lack of money, it wasn't his environment either that was at fault. It was him. Wherever he was, he would still be Charles Paris. And Charles Paris would always feel transitory, never quite committing himself to an environment, a community, perhaps even an identity. That was the reason he was an actor. So much easier to channel yourself into other personalities than to stand up and be counted on your own.

Anyway, he felt more at ease—or if not more at ease,

at least less challenged—living in anonymous surroundings, seeing as little of them as possible, and then ideally through a permanent haze of Bell's whiskey. That was just the way he was.

Having dispelled from his mind the idea of moving, Charles found it quickly filled with thoughts of Sippy Stokes's death, or as he preferred to think of it, Sippy Stokes's murder.

Maurice's words about the police still investigating encouraged this conjecture. Yes, it could have been an accident, but why should the shelves suddenly have toppled over when Sippy was in the props room? Why should she have been in the props room, anyway? And why should she have had the bad luck to be hit by a randomly falling object?

The idea of her having been hit by a carefully aimed object was much more attractive. And the idea that that object was the temporarily removed candlestick was even more appealing.

Charles thought back forty-eight hours and tried to remember the exact sequence of events.

On the Wednesday morning, when the studio broke for coffee after recording Russell Bentley's cutaway shot, Charles remembered seeing Sippy Stokes alive and well. She had turned down his casual invitation to join him in the canteen. It was only about half an hour later that he had found her body, still warm and bleeding, in the props room.

The actual coffee break had only been twenty minutes, but Charles thought it reasonable to assume that that was when the murder had taken place. Then the studio and its environs would have been almost deserted; to commit a murder once the cast and crew had returned would be much more risky.

But who could have been in the studio during the break to do the deed? Charles focused his memory, trying to reenvision who had been in the canteen and for how long.

Rick Landor hadn't been there at all. Nor had Russell Bentley. Nor, come to that, had W. T. Wintergreen and her sister. Any of them could have been anywhere during the break.

Will Parton had been in the canteen but been dragged away before the end of the break by Ben Docherty and Dilly Muirfield. However, their proposed script discussion hadn't taken place, so any of those three could in theory have gone back to the studio to dispose of Sippy Stokes.

Jimmy Sheet had left at the same time as Will, claiming he was going to look through some lines in his dressing room. But then, if he was planning a murder, he wouldn't have balked at lying about his intentions.

Mort Verdon had stayed chatting with Charles until after the end of the break, so he seemed to be in the clear, but the quiet A.S.M., Tony Rees, had left at the same time as Jimmy Sheet. And, Charles suddenly remembered, Tony Rees had looked very guilty when surprised around the back of the set, just before the discovery of Sippy's body. Yes, that young man certainly merited investigation.

But what motive might he have had to kill the actress?

What motive might any of them have had, come to that?

Charles scanned the possibilities:

Rick Landor was having an affair with Sippy Stokes and seemed angry that Jimmy Sheet was trying to ace him out.

If Jimmy Sheet was involved with her, maybe he had some motive of jealousy or anger.

Ben Docherty had already made the decision to sack the actress, which surely ruled out any reason for trying to get rid of her prematurely.

Russell Bentley was unhappy with the recording that they'd done so far, but even for someone with an ego as big as his, it was a little fanciful to imagine that he'd resort to murder to get the episode remade.

Dilly Muirfield and Will Parton appeared to have no possible motive for killing Sippy Stokes, unless they felt extremely strongly about the effect her dire performance was having on their series. And surely, though television people were notorious for how seriously they took television, that was going a bit far.

Oh, and then presumably W. T. Wintergreen and her sister might also have been snooping around the set during the coffee break. But again, except for the benefit of ridding the world of a dreadful actress, they didn't seem to have an obvious motive.

Insufficient information, Charles concluded. I'm going to have to find out a great deal more before I can start coming to any conclusions about the case. And do a lot more thinking.

But fortunately he was prevented from doing any more thinking at that moment by the ringing of the phone on the landing.

* * *

"Hello?"

"Oh, good morning. Is that Charles Paris?"

"Yes."

"This is Winifred Railton speaking."

"Oh."

His monosyllable must have revealed how little the name meant to him, because the elderly, cultured voice explained, "You probably know me better as W. T. Wintergreen."

"Oh, yes. Funny, I was just thinking about you."

"Nothing bad, I hope?"

"Ah. Well . . . um . . ." He couldn't really say that he'd been assessing her suitability as a murder suspect, could he? "No, no, of course not."

"Look, Mr. Paris, I was wondering if it would be possible for us to meet."

"Yes, I'm sure it would. But we'll be meeting on Monday at the read-through, anyway, won't we?"

"Oh, yes, I'll certainly be there. But I was meaning meet in a more private way. It's so impossible to talk on those occasions."

"Yes. Well, perhaps a drink after rehearsal . . ."

"I wondered if you would like to come to tea with me and my sister on Tuesday afternoon," W. T. Wintergreen said firmly.

"Oh. Um . . . Well, I'm not quite sure what the schedule—"

"I've checked. You won't be required for rehearsal on Tuesday afternoon."

"Well, then, what can I say? Yes, of course I'd be delighted. Where would you like to meet?"

W. T. Wintergreen had it all worked out. "If you come to our cottage at half past three, that will be fine."

"And where is your cottage?"

"Ham Common."

"Oh." Sounded to Charles a hell of a way to go for tea. Still, he'd said yes. And it could be rather interesting.

"I'll give you the precise address on Monday. Louisa and I will look forward to seeing you then. I trust you have a pleasant weekend. Good-bye, Mr. Paris."

Well, thought Charles as he put the phone down, what on earth was all that about?

On Saturday morning Charles rose late, more or less reassembled himself with coffee, and by half past eleven was feeling ready to go out to his local for a few pints and maybe even one of their range of Designer Ploughman's Lunches. What would it be today? A Brie Ploughman's? A Boursin Ploughman's? A Terrine de Canard Ploughman's? A Bratwurst and Sauerkraut Ploughman's?

He sometimes wondered what had happened to pub food in the last few years. In the old days, when you ordered a Ploughman's Lunch, you got a chunk of dry bread, a slab of hard cheese, a gold-wrapped packet of butter, with a tomato and maybe a pickled onion by way of garnish. Whereas now the Ploughmen really seemed to have moved up the social scale to become at least Gentlemen Farmers.

Charles blamed the Common Market. Most totally inexplicable developments in modern Britain had something to do with the Common Agricultural Policy.

It was while he was indulging these thoughts that he realized he was at that moment uniquely qualified to ring his wife. "When you're sober," Frances had said, and not a drop of alcohol had passed his lips for nearly twelve hours.

He rang her Highgate flat and was gratified to find her in. He felt suddenly very close to her. Yes, he had decided while the phone was ringing, they should meet up the next day for lunch. Sunday lunch, just like the old days. He could take her out somewhere on his W.E.T. loot. Or, better still, she might offer to cook lunch for him. Now that really would be like old times.

"See, Frances, here I am, ringing you at a reasonable time of day and stone-cold sober. What more could you ask?"

"A divorce?" she suggested, but her tone was not as hard as her words.

"You don't want one really, Frances. You love being unmarried to me."

"Ha. Ha. Anyway, tell me about this job you've got."

He told her. She was impressed. "Three-month contract—running character. You realize you're in danger of becoming a success, Charles Paris?"

"Oh, I don't think that'd ever happen," he said in mock self-deprecation.

"No, nor do I," Frances agreed dryly. "Still, I'm glad they're doing W. T. Wintergreen. I used to like her books."

"I have to confess I'd never heard of them until the job came up."

"They're good, if you like that sort of thing."

"Having read the scripts, I'm not sure that I do. They're totally unrealistic."

"That's part of their charm. Stanislas Braid is one of

those completely unbelievable superman-sleuths who know everything about everything. School of Lord Peter Wimsey. And he has these wonderful and totally unrealistic relationships with everyone around him. Blodd, the chauffeur . . . the delightfully innocent and deeply loved Christina. Yes, totally unbelievable, but comforting.''

"Hmm. I think I prefer my detective heroes a bit more realistic.''

"No, no. Couldn't disagree more. The last thing I want is reality muscling in and spoiling a good detective story. I'm a great believer in the 'Warm Bath' school of crime fiction—you know, books that are all snug and soothing and reassuring, books in which the Goodies are Good and the Baddies are Bad and you need never have a moment's anxiety about the fact that Good Will Triumph.''

"I find some of them a bit arch and mimsy-pimsy.''

"Wimsey—mimsy-pimsy?'' asked Frances in mock horror.

"Oh, shut up. When did W. T. Wintergreen write her books?''

"I don't know exactly. Maybe she still *is* writing them?''

"Surely not still about Stanislas Braid? Not still set back in the thirties? In that old country-house time warp?''

"No, perhaps not. I'm not sure. I know she published a few before the war, and at that time apparently they were spoken of in the same breath as Dorothy Sayers and Margery Allingham. Then I think she went on till . . . late fifties, maybe? I certainly haven't been aware of any new titles since then. But I'm really not up-to-date. Ages since I've read one. Mind you, they were very important during my adolescence. Read all of them then; it felt like dozens. I had these fantasies of marrying someone as suave and debonair and brilliant as Stanislas Braid.''

''Good heavens. Did you really?''

''Yes, I did. And look what I ended up with.''

''Thank you, Frances, for those few kind words. Anyway, you will no doubt be impressed to hear that I am going to have tea with W. T. Wintergreen herself on Tuesday.''

''Are you really?''

''Mm. Shall I tell her my wife's a fan?''

''Yes, by all means.''

''Right, I will.'' A silence hung between them. ''Frances, I was actually ringing to see if we could meet up.''

''Ah.'' She didn't sound one hundred percent welcoming to the idea.

''We did talk about it.''

''*You* talked about it.''

''Yes. Well?''

''When do you want to meet?''

''Soon. Sooner the better.''

''Well, I'm leaving this afternoon to go and stay with some friends for the weekend.''

''Oh.'' He felt a stab of disappointment.

''School as usual next week, and at the moment I find I'm too tired really to enjoy going out weekday evenings. Next weekend, perhaps?''

''Yes.'' Now he was near to clinching the date, Charles felt unaccountably gauche and unwilling to firm it up. Almost as nervous as he had felt in such circumstances during his teens. And this was with his own wife, for God's sake. ''Well, look, I'm not absolutely certain of the schedule on the series for this week. They add odd days of filming and things. I think next weekend'd be all right, but can I get back to you on it?''

''Yes, fine,'' said Frances. But she made it sound as if it didn't really matter to her a great deal whether he did or not.

He had his designer lunch in the pub. Dutch Rollmop Ploughman's. That really was taking the Common Agricultural Policy too far, he reckoned. Still, it gave him a good thirst for the beer.

He felt pretty good, really. Almost content. There was no one in the pub he knew more than to nod at, but that suited him fine. And of course no one recognized him as an actor. He wondered idly if that situation would change once *Stanislas Braid* was being funneled into the nation's sitting rooms. Six months thence, if he sat on the same chair, would he be aware of people on the fringes of his vision nudging each other and whispering, ''Isn't that . . . ?'' The idea seemed ridiculous. But the extrovert in Charles Paris, the part that made him an actor, wasn't wholly repelled by it.

He picked up a tabloid newspaper that someone had left on the table and glanced through it. World news didn't seem to get any less depressing. In fact, now it seemed to him that the bits that weren't depressing or horrifying were just boring. He tried to remember when he'd last read something in a newspaper that had *interested* him. A very long time ago. Dear, oh, dear, he was becoming a cynical, dessicated old stick.

His eye was caught by a familiar name on the gossip-column page, and he read the snide little paragraph with fascination.

"Everyone knows there's nothing wrong with gilded warbler Jimmy Sheet's marriage. He keeps telling us that after the threatened earthquakes of last year it's as solid as a rock. So no doubt lovable cockney Jim has told his wife all about the mystery brunette he squired to Stringfellow's on Tuesday night. Otherwise one might say that Jimmy, now turning his attentions from music to acting, is in danger of being *caught in the act!*"

It was a typical piece of nudging copy, but it confirmed what Mort Verdon had told Charles. And confirmed Sippy Stokes's fairly lowly profile in the entertainment industry. The columnist had presumably tried without success to identify her. Just as well, from Jimmy Sheet's point of view, that no one had made the connection between the mystery girl at Stringfellow's and the dead actress whose photograph was all over Thursday's newspapers.

Still, the paragraph offered an intriguing new sidelight on the character of Jimmy Sheet. Hmm, thought Charles, maybe newspapers do sometimes contain news that's interesting.

CHAPTER
SEVEN

Charles sometimes wondered who found television rehearsal rooms. Was there an elite band of dedicated men whose sole mission was to scour London for boys' clubs and rugby clubs and church halls and drill halls that passed the stringent tests of suitability for their purpose? How many potential venues were rejected on the grounds of being too comfortable or insufficiently dispiriting? How many were rejected for being too convenient for public transport or because they had adequate parking? How many failed selection because they were actually congenial places in which to spend one's time?

The conjectural band of searchers had clearly excelled themselves when they found the St. John Chrysostom Mission for Vagrants Lesser Hall, in which the rehearsals for *Stanislas Braid* took place. This was the apotheosis of the television rehearsal room, the one for which every other hall in London must have been rejected.

Situated a good twenty minutes' walk from the nearest tube station, jammed in an alley between a cement works and a timber yard, whose lorries were a perpetual hazard to anyone foolish enough to risk leaving their car outside, the Lesser Hall's high windows were so begrimed that what light did filter through had an unhealthy, diluted pallor about it. The lights inside, kept constantly switched on, apologetically illuminated walls the color of baby shit. As Charles looked around the room on the Monday morning of the second read-through, he realized with delight that he had finally found a context in which to use one of his favorite words: "fuscous."

The only bright colors in the room, apart from the clothes of the cast and production team, were the strips of variously colored tape with which the outlines of the different sets had been marked on the floor by assiduous stage managers. But these were largely covered by the long chain of tables, surrounded by chairs, at which the read-through was to take place.

W. T. Wintergreen—or Winifred Railton—had acknowledged Charles with an inclination of her head but made no reference to their conversation of the previous Friday. She had a script open on her lap and, with her sister, Louisa, as ever, close beside her, was deep in conversation with Dilly Muirfield. From the expression on the script editor's face, she was getting yet more complaints that the script of this episode, "The Italian Stiletto Murder," had diverged too far from the original book and that, as Louisa Railton recurrently complained in fierce whispers to her sister, "Stanislas Braid just wouldn't *do* that."

Charles spared a few moments of sympathy for Dilly Muirfield's role. She was the mediator; it was she who had to listen to the endless cavils of the writer of the books, the writers of the scripts, the stars, the producer, and the director. She then, rather as the floor manager did in the studio, had to translate the complaints into acceptable demands for the people against whom they were made.

Charles had heard this process in action more than once. He had heard Russell Bentley denouncing the script to Dilly with the words "It's a load of shit—the work of an absolute incompetent. I mean, the character of Stanislas Braid virtually disappears for the whole middle of the episode."

And he had heard Dilly relaying the message to Will Parton in conciliatory tones: "I was just wondering whether it might be *better* if we inserted a little extra scene for Stanislas Braid in the middle here, you know, just to remind the audience how he's proceeding with his investigation?"

He had also heard Will Parton's response to this suggestion, and though the object of the writer's vilification had been Russell Bentley, it was Dilly Muirfield who had to listen to all the foul language. She really was in a no-win situation.

Working for a producer like Ben Docherty, whose daily Jekyll and Hyde act made him quite capable of spending the whole afternoon reversing all the decisions he had made in the morning, can't have made the script editor's job any easier.

* * *

What was striking about that morning in the St. John Chrysostom Mission for Vagrants Lesser Hall was how little impact the death of Sippy Stokes had made on the production. Rick Landor, the one person who might have been personally affected, was not there, and for the new director it was ancient history, something that had happened the week before, nothing to do with him.

The new director was only in his late twenties. This was his first major production, and he was very much on his dignity, determined to impose his authority on the proceedings. His mind was too full of the professional challenges of the coming fortnight to have any room for thoughts of the previous week's death.

But the rest of the cast and production team, those who had been working with the dead girl only a few days before, seemed equally unaffected. The ripples caused by her death had quickly smoothed themselves out, and the surface of the production was just as it had been before.

Or, to be truthful, it was rather better than it had been before. Previously, the knowledge of what a bad actress Sippy Stokes was had infected everyone with a kind of unease, the feeling that her incompetence might be sabotaging the chances of their series.

The new girl, Joanne Rhymer, it was immediately evident, would be a very different proposition. For a start, she looked much better for the part. Sippy Stokes, though an attractive girl, had had a gypsy, almost tarty quality about her. Her dark hair and sensuous lips had seemed too knowing for the innocent Christina, and the woodenness of her performance had given some of her lines an unwanted air of innuendo, as if she were sending up their naïveté.

But Joanne Rhymer, although dressed as fashionably as befitted a twenty-year-old actress, had about her a timeless quality. Her face was heart-shaped, and her blond hair showed off flashes of auburn even in the muted lighting of the St. John Chrysostom Mission for Vagrants Lesser Hall. She had a trim figure that would suit the range of thirties dresses so painstakingly assembled by Wardrobe.

Above all, she had about her an air of credible innocence. The potentially twee lines of Christina, the cloying relationship between her and her father, might become almost believable when expressed by this child-woman.

Charles couldn't help speculating about how much her character reflected the innocence of her appearance. His conversation with Maurice had reminded him of Gwen Rhymer's fabled nymphomania. Was it by any chance a characteristic that the daughter had inherited? Was he looking at another Blue Nun in the making?

You're a disgusting, prurient old sod, he told himself. Real classic dirty old man. But this self-administered admonition didn't stop his speculations. The trouble was, you see, he had once been the beneficiary of Gwen Rhymer's "proclivities," and while not approving of her behavior or reputation, he couldn't help remembering that he had enjoyed the experience enormously. So he felt justified in having more than a passing interest in her daughter's character.

As soon as the read-through started, it was clear that Joanne Rhymer's talent was equal to her looks. She brought a kind of resilience to the character's naïveté. Lines that looked hopelessly sentimental on the page managed, through her delivery, to become charming.

Everyone in the rehearsal room was aware of the

contrast from the first read-through. At that stage they had suspected that Sippy Stokes was, like a lot of actresses, just a bad reader. The full deficiency of her talent had not then been exposed. But it had still made for an edgy atmosphere.

With Joanne Rhymer in the part, though, everyone could relax. Charles watched as she read her first scene and saw the relief growing on various faces around the table.

Will Parton looked positively triumphant, finally vindicated in the knowledge that his lines would work if played in the right way. W. T. Wintergreen and Louisa also beamed; for the first time they seemed to be happy about the way one of the *Stanislas Braid* characters was being portrayed. Russell Bentley seemed at ease, too. He probably wasn't aware of why he felt better; the habit of not noticing what the rest of the cast did prevented him from realizing how well his lines were being fed to him; but at last he seemed able to play the part of Russell Bentley.

And Ben Docherty's face glowed with benevolence, as if he were a proud father watching the performance of his favorite daughter.

Yes, there was no doubt about it. Joanne Rhymer's performance worked. She *was* Christina Braid.

Except, of course, she wasn't. She was Elvira Braid, just back from finishing school in Switzerland. Her sister, Christina, thanks to the inspired invention of Will Parton, had "gone to Paris to nurse an old school friend recovering from a nasty bout of influenza."

They got through the whole of the first Stanislas Braid/ Christina scene before Russell Bentley interrupted the reading. "Look, there's something wrong here."

"Sorry, could we read straight through?" said the new director. "We're doing this on the watch. We'll pick up any notes afterward."

"No, this is important. We've got to sort it out before we go on."

"I'm sorry. Read-through first," insisted the director, unaware that he was entering his first battle of wills with his star.

"No," said Russell Bentley firmly.

The P.A. gave a short-tempered sigh and clicked off her stopwatch.

"Look, I'm the director," said the new director, "and if I say we continue the read-through, then we continue the read-through."

"No," Russell Bentley repeated.

"Come on, you're a professional actor. Surely you know how to behave at a rehearsal?"

This was dangerous ground. The worst insult that can be thrown at an actor is the accusation that he's unprofessional. And for a new director to throw it at his star on a first read-through showed a lack of diplomacy that verged on the suicidal.

Russell Bentley's face flushed with anger. "Are you saying that I'm not—"

Ben Docherty realized the gravity of the situation and fulfilled his producer's role by interrupting. "Now just a minute. Don't let's get heated about this. I think Russell may have a point."

"I'm the director," the new director insisted doggedly, "and I say we should get on with the read-through."

"Well, I'm the producer," said Ben Docherty, "and I say we should hear what Russell has to say first."

"All right." The new director flung his script petulantly down on the table. "If you're one of those producers who constantly undermines his director's authority..."

Ben Docherty didn't rise to this bait. Instead, he turned to his star in a conciliatory manner and said, "Now, what was your point, Russell?"

"Simply this, Ben. This lovely young girl—what was your name again, dear?"

"Joanne."

"Yes, Joanne... is playing a part just like that of Christina, my daughter, and yet—" Russell continued, repeating for emphasis—"and *yet* we keep referring to the character as 'Elvira.'"

"Yes, Russell, and you know the reasons for that. Look, I agree, the characters are virtually interchangeable, but that makes things even simpler. All you have to do is to say the different name."

"It's not just that. I also have a bit of meaningless drivel about finishing schools in Switzerland and friends with influenza. Why can't I just cut all that and call the character Christina?"

"You know why. Because we've already got two-thirds of an episode in the can with a different actress playing Christina."

"A rather dreadful actress, I may say."

"That, Russell, is a matter of opinion. All I know is that W.E.T. can't afford to write off what we've already done on the first episode."

"Well, I think they should."

Charles had been aware of considerable muttering between the two Railton sisters during this exchange but was surprised when W. T. Wintergreen's voice was suddenly heard, firmly announcing, "I couldn't agree more."

The producer turned wearily to the crime writer. "Look, W. T. . . . Miss Wintergreen . . . Miss Railton." He was always at a loss as to how to address her. "I know it would be very nice if we could just scrap the last two weeks' work, but I'm afraid it's a matter of economics."

"No, it's not. It's a matter of what the public expect from a series called *Stanislas Braid*. My readers are already going to be deeply distressed and disappointed by the number of gratuitous changes which have been made to my books, but when it comes to changing the names of one of the major characters, one of the best-loved characters indeed, the character of Christina . . . well, I just don't think they'll stand for it."

"Think yourself lucky they haven't changed her sex and made her black," Will Parton muttered to no one in particular.

"Miss Railton," Ben Docherty began, homing in on the name with infinite patience, "I'm rather afraid you may flatter yourself about the power of your readers. You say they won't stand for it. . . . Well, how do you suppose they're going to express the fact that they don't stand for it? Anyway, Miss Railton, we're not talking about books. As I've told you many times before, we're talking about television. A whole different ball game. Do you realize that *one* showing of *one* of the episodes of this series will be seen by more people than all the readers of all your books put together? Most of the viewers, I'm afraid, will never have heard of W. T. Wintergreen. A large number of them probably never read books, anyway. So, for them, whether a character is called Christina or Elvira will not make the blindest bit of difference.''

"But it makes all the difference in the world!" This outburst came from Louisa Railton, so incensed by what was being said that she forgot her customary shyness.

Russell Bentley renewed his attack on the beleaguered producer. "Listen, Ben, I have a reputation in television. When members of the public see my name on a credit in the *T.V. Times* or whatever, they know what kind of thing to expect.''

Yes, your inimitable impersonation of Russell Bentley, thought Charles mischievously.

"In other words, what I'm saying is, I've got my own standards. And I don't feel that anything we recorded last week was up to those standards.''

"But we did all that filming," Ben Docherty wailed. "I mean, the costs if we do write it off are just terrifying.''

"Not as terrifying as putting that rubbish out. I mean, since when has W.E.T. been in the business of putting out substandard productions?''

"Since the company was formed," Will Parton mouthed silently to Charles, who tried not to giggle.

"Anyway, we didn't get the whole episode recorded," Russell Bentley continued. "You're going to have to extend the schedule to pick up the extra scenes, and since you've got to rebook everyone for that, you might as well just remake the episode.''

"Not necessarily.''

"What do you mean?''

"He means," Will Parton suddenly interposed, "that he might not have to rebook *everyone*.''

Russell Bentley looked at the producer, who was

gazing with hatred at the writer. "That was a private conversation we had, Will."

"Well, we may as well make it public, because I'm afraid your little idea isn't going to work, Ben. I'm prepared to go through quite a few contortions as a writer, but this time you're just asking too much."

"What 'little idea' is this we're talking about?" asked Russell Bentley quietly.

"There's no need to tell him," the producer snapped. "Come on, we should be getting on with this read-through."

But Will Parton, having decided on his course, was not going to be deflected from it. "Ben's idea," he said coolly, "was that I should do a major rewrite on the episode—a major salvage operation—a major evisceration, if you like. That I should somehow incorporate the scenes that are in the can and rewrite the rest of the story in a way that only involved rebooking two artistes."

"Only two!" said Russell Bentley.

"But that would make nonsense of my story," objected W. T. Wintergreen, appalled by the perfidy of the suggestion.

"Oh, yes," said Will ironically, "it'd make nonsense of the story. It'd make a dreadful television program that I'd be ashamed to have my credit on . . . that all of us would be ashamed to have our credits on. Oh, yes, but think of the money it'd save."

There was a silence. All eyes were fixed on Ben Docherty.

But the producer's eyes were fixed on Will Parton. Fixed with an expression of deep loathing.

CHAPTER
<u>EIGHT</u>

After this confrontation the read-through continued, but the "atmosphere" it had engendered remained in the St. John Chrysostom Mission for Vagrants Lesser Hall. As soon as they had reached the end of the script, Russell Bentley turned straight back to Ben Docherty and reiterated, "It's going to make a lot more sense if we do just change the girl's name back to Christina. Cut all that heavy-handed garbage in the first scene about finishing schools. It'll make the whole thing flow much more smoothly."

"But that will mean committing myself to scrapping last week's work. So long as we change the name, we have at least got the option. See what kind of magic Will can work on the script."

"I can't do magic," the writer announced flatly. "I

can manage the occasional conjuring trick, but magic—forget it.''

"Well . . ."

"Mr. Docherty," said W. T. Wintergreen, "you really must call the character Christina. You've just no idea how important it is. So much depends on the characters having the right names."

"A lot may depend from your *readers'* point of view," the producer conceded, deciding that W. T. Wintergreen was an easier target to hit back at than Russell Bentley, "but so far as I'm concerned, a name is just a name."

"Then you've clearly never written anything," the old girl responded spiritedly.

"He's *re*written a good few things," Will Parton muttered.

"If you had," W. T. Wintergreen continued, "you would know the care that must go into the selection of the proper name for a character. Sometimes I spend whole weeks before I start a book getting the names right."

"I don't think the viewing public are as hypersensitive about it as you are."

"I'm not concerned with the viewing public."

"Well, I am. In fact, it's my sole concern. It's my job to be concerned about the viewing public."

"The fact remains that the character of Christina is a 'Christina' and not an 'Elvira.' "

"Yes, come on, let's just call her Christina and be done with it," said Russell Bentley.

"No, I'm sorry, Russell. I'll have to give this some thought."

"Look, Ben, if you were reckoning just to pick up the

odd scene over the next two and a half months so that you can cobble together a first episode, forget it."

"But we can't afford to extend the schedule."

"I'm afraid I can never take it that seriously when a commercial television company pleads poverty, Ben."

"It's true. Then there are problems with booking studios. And you're not available after the end of this contract."

"I will make myself available," Russell Bentley announced grandly. "If that is the only problem in the way of remaking the first episode, I will guarantee to make myself available."

"Oh, well..." For the first time Ben Docherty's resolve appeared to weaken. "I'll have to check the feasibility of it with Contracts and studio and Outside Broadcast facilities."

Russell Bentley beamed. Once again he appeared to be achieving what gave him the greatest satisfaction in life—getting his own way. "Everything's possible, Ben, even in television."

The producer chewed his lip unhappily.

Then the new director chipped in, demonstrating once again that whatever his skills in framing artistic camera shots, he had a few things to learn in the diplomacy department. "But you're going to have to give us a decision very soon. I mean, I'm the director of this show, and I can't fart around with script changes at this point."

"I'll have to check a lot of things out," said Ben Docherty, too dispirited even to notice the insubordination.

"Well, you'd better do it bloody quickly. If we're going to cut the finishing-school crap, we may have to add something to make up the time."

"Oh, I'm sure you won't need to," Will Parton drawled. "Most directors can easily make up time with a few *artistic* shots that slow down the pace and add nothing to the story."

He spoke with the bitter experience of a writer who had seen too many of his favorite lines cut to make way for directorial self-indulgence, but the new director's keenness to get on with rehearsal prevented the outbreak of another argument.

"As I say, I'll think about it," Ben Docherty confirmed. Then he looked at his watch. "I'd better get back to the office."

Charles Paris felt certain that the producer's route back to his office would take in some convenient pub.

"Right." Russell Bentley turned to the new director the minute Ben Docherty was out of the room. "Let's take that as read then. We cut all the finishing-school garbage, and you, my dear— What was your name again?"

"Joanne."

"Of course, Joanne. Well, you, Joanne, will be referred to as Christina throughout."

Everyone in the St. John Chrysostom Mission for Vagrants Lesser Hall seemed very happy with this hijacking of their producer's authority. For some, like W. T. Wintergreen and Louisa Railton, the satisfaction derived from artistic considerations. For others, like Charles Paris, its roots were more basic. If the schedule for making the *Stanislas Braid* series was to be extended, that meant not only that unemployment would be staved off by another couple of weeks but also that he would receive yet another healthy W.E.T. fee.

Yes, it was very satisfactory all around. The production could continue as if Sippy Stokes had never existed. And it would be a much better production for her absence. So everyone, with the possible exception of Ben Docherty, had benefited from her death.

But had anyone actually benefited enough to justify their murdering her?

"Here we are, boofle. Schedules." Mort Verdon bustled up to him, a sheaf of photocopied sheets draped over his arm. "Going on your travels, Charles."

"What do you mean?"

"Filming for the next episode. Actually going away."

"What—you mean locations farther than half a mile from W.E.T. House?"

His question only slightly exaggerated the situation. Like most television companies, W.E.T. had its little repertoire of favorite locations, and the reason for their popularity was their proximity to the company headquarters. Because W.E.T. House was situated in Lisson Avenue, N.W.1, a disproportionate amount of the action in W.E.T. series seemed to be located in that area. Television car chases took place on the Westway. Television crooks lived in Maida Vale mansion blocks. Television drug pushers haunted Church Street Market. Television lovers entwined at London Zoo or on the towpath of Regent's Park Canal. And Regent's Park itself was transformed into an incredible variety of television exteriors, from the Dust Bowl of the American Midwest to the steaming jungles of Borneo.

Mort Verdon nodded in reply to Charles's question.

"Oh, yes, boofle. And you'd better pack your bucket and spade. You're going to the seaside."

"How exciting. Where to? How long for?"

"You're going to the Isle of Purbeck."

"Oh." Charles looked blank. "Remind me."

"Dorset. It's not a real island. At least not for a few millennia. More sort of *pen*insula than insular these days."

"Name some towns."

"Swanage, Studland, Corfe Castle."

"Oh, right. I know where you mean. Just didn't know it was called the Isle of Purbeck."

"Learn a little something every day, boofle."

"I certainly try to. When is this?"

"Ep. three. Rick's next production. Week's rehearsal starting fortnight today and travel down the following Sunday to start filming Monday morning. Travel back Tuesday evening, rest day Wednesday, studio Thurs and Fri."

"Terrific." Though he found the actual process of filming deeply boring, the prospect of forty-eight hours of hotels and location catering was very appealing. "W.E.T. really pushing the boat out."

"Hard to avoid it with an episode called 'The Seashore Murder,'" said Mort Verdon dryly.

"Hmm. Why is it I never get involved in episodes called "The Barbados Murder' or 'The Acapulco Murder' or 'The Seychelles Murder'?"

"Don't be greedy, Charles. You'll have a lovely time in Swanage."

"Oh, I'm sure I will. Nice hotel?"

"Of course."

"Great."

"All the facilities you might require—bar, restaurant, another bar, sauna, yet another bar. Ideal bed-hopping territory."

"Oh, I think I'm a bit old for that sort of thing."

"Not what I've heard, Charles Paris."

Charles chuckled, as if to dismiss the idea. Mind you, he was rather flattered by it. Even slightly excited.

"Anyway, boofle . . ." Mort Verdon leaned forward in mock-seriousness and laid his hand on Charles's. "If you want to hop into my bed, all I can advise is, book early to avoid the crowds."

"Okay." Charles grinned back. "Thanks. I'll bear that in mind."

The rehearsal schedule for the next three days was confirmed, and Charles was not called again till Wednesday morning. So, as W. T. Wintergreen had told him, he would be free on Tuesday afternoon.

Before the new director started blocking Russell Bentley and Joanne Rhymer's first scene, there was a break, during which the girls from Wardrobe went around, checking measurements with the cast members only appearing in that episode and discussing choice of costumes with the regular performers. Since Sergeant Clump never appeared in anything other than his uniform—though Will Parton had threatened to get a wacky scene of the village bobby in his underwear into the last episode— Charles was free to do whatever he wanted to do.

What he did want to do was, unsurprisingly, to go and have a drink, and he looked around the St. John Chrysostom Mission for Vagrants Lesser Hall for a suitable accomplice in this enterprise. If there wasn't anyone around, Charles would not revise his plans in any major way; but drinking with someone else always did give him a spurious feeling of righteousness.

Jimmy Sheet had also been released from rehearsal for the rest of the day, and since Blodd, like Sergeant Clump, was rarely seen in anything other than his uniform, he did not need any discussions with Wardrobe either.

"Fancy a drink?" Charles asked diffidently.

"Where?" asked the former pop star.

"There's a pub just down the road. Pretty grotty, but the beer's okay."

Jimmy Sheet grimaced. "Don't like pubs, really, these days. Don't get no privacy; people keep recognizing me."

"Oh." This was one of the hazards of show business that Charles's career had not yet had to negotiate. Still, maybe when Sergeant Clump was a familiar face in the nation's living rooms, all that would change. Somehow he doubted it.

"Tell you what, though," said Jimmy Sheet. "We could go to this club I know. Have a quick snifter there."

"Well, fine, if that's all right. Where is it?"

"Not far. We'll go in the motor." His cockney glottal stop completely removed the "t" from the word. He pronounced it "mo-ah."

The "mo-ah" turned out to be a two-seater silver Mercedes. It had a personalized "JS" number plate. Not for the first time, Charles reflected on the contradiction he had encountered in the personality of many "celebrities," who, while constantly asserting their desperate desire for privacy, drove everywhere in vehicles that advertised their presence.

The car was parked athwart double yellow lines opposite the St. John Chrysostom Mission for Vagrants. Jimmy Sheet wasn't going to put his "mo-ah" at risk from the swinging lorries of the cement works or the timber yard. And the risk of traffic wardens clearly didn't worry him. Without comment, he removed the ticket from the windscreen and shoved it into the glove compartment to join a pile of others.

As soon as they were under way, Jimmy Sheet picked up the car phone and punched out a number from the memory. "Won't be a sec., Charles. Oh, hello, love, it's me. How's things? Yeah, great. No, I'm not called again till tomorrow. Sure. Yes, well, I'll be back round four, I reckon. Four, half past. No, just going off for a drink at the club with one of the cast. No, love, of course not. He's a bloke. Charles Paris. No, well, he— You might recognize the face. Of course I am. Say hello, Charles."

Charles looked in amazement at the telephone thrust in front of him.

"It's the wife," Jimmy Sheet said, as if that explained everything. "Sharon. Go on, say hello."

"Oh, hello, Sharon," Charles obeyed, though he felt somewhat bewildered.

Jimmy Sheet took the phone back. "See? Told you. Okay, then, see you later, love. Love you. 'Bye."

He returned the phone to its rest and made no comment on the bizarre incident that had just taken place.

Jimmy Sheet's club was on a small street not far from Grosvenor Square. Once again he pulled the Mercedes to a halt on double yellow lines directly outside the entrance and, pausing only to don dark glasses, got out, clearly intending to leave it there.

"Aren't you worried about getting clamped?" asked Charles tentatively.

"Nah. There's this service that sorts it out for you. And I've got an account with this limo company what'll send one round pronto to take me home."

Money, it seemed, was not a problem for Mr. Sheet.

His club looked expensive, too. But whereas Charles had been expecting something rather glitzy and American, a place full of girls with variegated hair where no drink was served without a cluster of umbrellas in it, the reception into which Jimmy Sheet ushered him was very restrained and patrician. Paneled walls and marble pillars, much nearer the Athenaeum than the Groucho.

The porter, who would have been well cast as a minor retainer in an episode of *Stanislas Braid*, good-afternoon-Mr.-Sheeted him, and Jimmy magnanimously asked after the porter's family while signing Charles in. It was interesting to see how quickly new money absorbed the habits of old money.

In the dark wood-and-leather peace of the bar, Jimmy Sheet greeted a few pin-striped gentlemen who showed no resentment of his open-necked shirt and oyster-gray leather jacket. They were too much gentlemen even to show resentment of Charles's neolithic sports jacket.

A waiter, so discreet as to be almost invisible, took their orders for a large Bell's and a spritzer. Jimmy Sheet popped a stuffed olive in his mouth, chewed it, and asked, "How'd you think it's going, then?"

"Not too bad," said Charles cautiously. "Rather better as of this morning than it was last week."

"Yeah." Jimmy Sheet nodded reflectively but did not pick up the cue to talk about Sippy Stokes. "Hope it'll be all right. The agent said it'd be a good series for me to do. Don't want to end up in a bummer."

Charles tried to imagine what it must be like to move in a world where your agent recommends shows that would be "good for you to do" rather than one where you grabbed anything that was offered.

"I'm sure it'll be all right," he said automatically. "Because actually this is your first big acting break, isn't it?"

"Could say that," Jimmy Sheet agreed. "Mind you, 'break' makes it sound like it was accidental. I mean, this was a calculated career move."

"Ah."

"Well, I mean, I could've kept on with the singing, but, you know, last couple of singles didn't get as high up the charts as the ones before, and I always reckoned to get out of that while I was still on top. It's all only means to an end, isn't it?"

"Is it?" asked Charles.

"Oh, sure. I done the singing because, you know, gives you a good international profile, but I never was going to stay with it. I mean, the money's there if you want to. Go into cabaret, you know, keep recycling the old hits—you can do that till the cows come home. But that was never how I wanted my career to pan out."

"No?"

"Nah. Anyway, all that traveling. You know, I reckon I done my bit on the touring front. Need something that doesn't take me away from home so much. Like to spend more time with Sharon and the kids."

"Actors do a lot of touring and location stuff."

"Oh, sure. But in the music business, you got to do it to keep up your profile. In acting, you know, you can choose your work."

Can you? thought Charles. First I've heard of it.

"And the acting, you know, you can keep it going, fit it round other things, business commitments and that."

"Really?"

"Yeah. I mean, again television's only another kind of staging post."

"Is it?"

"I'm just doing this series to, you know, like remind the public I'm not just a singer, I'm a good actor, and all. Kind of reestablish me in the public's mind in a different role."

"I see."

"Not going to stay with the television."

"Why not?"

"Well, it's not sort of international."

"I thought it could be. I thought it was becoming increasingly international."

"Yeah, but not at the same level as the music business or feature films."

"Well . . ."

"Apart from anything else, the money's peanuts, isn't it?"

Since the three months of the *Stanislas Braid* contract would be the best-paid three months of his life, Charles didn't feel qualified to reply to this.

"No, as I say," Jimmy Sheet went on, "it's feature films I'm going into in the long term."

"Oh, really?"

"Might do some theaters as well. . . . You know, if the right part comes up on Broadway, that kind of number."

Charles kept wondering why all this didn't sound unconvincing. He had heard similar dreams expressed by any number of actors, and his normal reaction was, all sounds great; you just wait till you get out into the *real* world, sonny. But Jimmy Sheet spoke with such assurance that he made his plans sound more like business decisions than pipe dreams. He seemed to be in no doubt that he would be able to follow his proposed career path, and Charles found himself equally convinced.

"What do you put your money in?" Jimmy Sheet asked suddenly.

"I beg your pardon?" said Charles.

"Your money—what's it in?"

"Erm . . ." Difficult question to answer, really. The truth—I haven't got any—sounded just too pathetic and self-pitying. "Oh, this and that."

"Mm. Spread the investment—something to be said for that, certainly. I got most of my dosh in property."

"Have you?"

"Yeah. Don't think you can ultimately lose with property."

"No. No, I suppose not. As Mark Twain said, 'Buy land, my son, they are not making any more.' "

"Who?"

"Mark Twain."

"Don't know him." Jimmy Sheet restlessly picked up another olive and flicked it into his mouth. "Got some property in the States, bit in Australia, quite a lot here in England."

"Ah."

"Well, you got to do something with it, haven't you?"

"Yes, yes."

Jimmy Sheet winked at the waiter, who ghosted up with more drinks. Charles decided it might be timely to move the conversation away from money, about which he'd never had the opportunity to know anything, to what he was really interested in.

"Terrible business last week, wasn't it?"

"What's that, then?" asked Jimmy.

"Sippy Stokes."

"Oh, yeah, yeah."

"Dreadful when something like that happens. You know, you feel you should have done more."

"Done more like what?"

"Got to know her better, perhaps."

"Why?"

"Well, when someone dies—"

"People die all the time."

"Yes, but when it's someone you know—"

"You just said you didn't know her."

Jimmy Sheet certainly wasn't making the conversation easy. "No, I mean . . ." Charles floundered on. "What I mean is, you just feel it's kind of a waste."

"Not a waste of an actress, certainly."

"Perhaps not. But a waste of a person."

"Maybe to the people who were close to her."

"Do you know who was close to her?"

Jimmy Sheet's eyes narrowed. "Well, I gather Rick Landor wasn't averse to giving her one every now and then."

"I suppose that's how she got the part."

"Can't think of any other reason. No, old Ben nearly

bust a gut when he heard about it. They'd done most of the major casting, and he was still dithering about who was going to play Christina—mind you, I think he'd got that Joanne bird in mind from the start. Then suddenly he hears Rick's pulled a fast one and put through the booking for his little bit on the side.''

"Couldn't Ben have put a stop to it?"

"Contract had gone out. He'd have had to pay her off for the series. And we saw this morning just how keen he is on writing things off.''

"Yes. Mind you, he had decided to pay her off after the first episode, anyway.''

"Had he?"

Quickly, Charles filled Jimmy in on what Will had told him in the bar after Sippy's death.

"Shit,'' said the singer at the end of the account. "That Ben Docherty can be a really nasty operator.''

"Yes. It's amazing that Sippy didn't hear from someone what he was planning.''

"Well, she didn't. She didn't have a clue on the Tuesday night, anyway.''

Jimmy Sheet had given something away there, and Charles pounced on it. "Oh, really? Did you see her on the Tuesday night?''

"What? No. No. Just at the end of the filming, you know, just had a chat.''

Charles would have recognized that the man was lying even if he hadn't known of his visit with the "mystery brunette'' to Stringfellow's.

"So you weren't one of the people who was close to her?''

"No. No, course I wasn't.'' Jimmy Sheet was becoming heated. "Shit, just because you've worked in the pop business, everybody thinks you're bloody bonking everything in sight. Look, all right, in what I do, things I've done, there's always been girls around. But I'm a happily married man. I got Sharon and the kids. Okay, in the past there may have been the odd flutter, but that's all finished—got it?"

It didn't take a very advanced student of psychology to recognize that the vehemence of this defense was totally disproportionate to the hint of an accusation that Charles had made. Nor to identify it as the operation of a guilty conscience.

As if to reinforce that impression—which hardly needed reinforcing—the ectoplasmic waiter suddenly materialized at Jimmy's side and murmured discreetly that Mr. Sheet's wife was on the telephone.

Checking up on him, Charles thought as the harassed husband went off to take the call. There was something amiss with Jimmy Sheet's marriage. His wife was a neurotically jealous woman, and she didn't trust him. As the newspaper gossip column had hinted, she could well be the sort to divorce him and take away his beloved children if she caught a whiff of any other extramarital excursions.

Taking Sippy Stokes out to Stringfellow's on the night before her death might well qualify under that heading.

Fine, so long as it remained secret. But it was a risky thing to do. Mort Verdon had seen them there. Any number of other people might have seen them there. It was only luck that the newspaper columnist hadn't been able to identify the "mystery brunette."

Anyway, suppose Sippy Stokes didn't want it to remain

secret? Suppose she had threatened to tell the lovely Sharon what had happened?

Then Jimmy Sheet might well feel that Sippy Stokes needed to be silenced.

CHAPTER
NINE

"Oh, hello, Charles. It's Maurice."

"*You* ringing *me?* Good heavens, what's happened?"

"Availability check."

"Good God, there's no stopping them at the moment. Is it the National Theatre again? I don't know, that lot just won't take no for an answer. Oh, well, I suppose if they *insist* on my giving my Lear, I can't really say no, can I?"

"Ha. Ha. You're in a very chirpy mood this bright Tuesday morning, aren't you? What's got into you?"

"I think it must be employment. I had forgotten how it felt to have things to do in the gaps between sleeping. And now my agent being flooded with availability checks..."

"One's hardly a flood, Charles."

"What about the two you had last Thursday?"

"What? Oh, yes. Yes, of course, I'd forgotten those."

But the pause between the "What?" and the "Oh,

yes" had been too long. Maurice had given himself away. As Charles had suspected, the availability checks of the previous week had been pure fabrication.

"Anyway, who wants to know my availability?"

"W.E.T."

"Hey, how about that? Success breeds success. What is it? Supporting artiste given his own series? New spin-off called *Sergeant Clump Investigates*? Or are they asking me to appear as a well-loved W.E.T. personality on some wacky, tacky game show?"

He offered these suggestions as jokes, but only partly as jokes. No actor can suppress that secret hope that one day, it really is all going to happen for him.

"It's none of that, Charles. It's still *Stanislas Braid*."

"Are they committing themselves to the second series already?"

"No, they're adding some extra dates to this series to pick up the episode they lost last week."

"Ah, yes. Yes, of course." So Ben Docherty had finally given in to the pressures around him. Sippy Stokes was to be erased completely from the series of *Stanislas Braid*. Russell Bentley had had his own way yet again.

"That's good news, Maurice. When is it? How're they doing it?"

"Just tacking a fortnight on to the end of this series. I mean, that's assuming everyone can make the dates. As I say, it's only an availability check at the moment. Presumably, if any of the regulars are committed elsewhere, they'll have to rethink. I mean, Russell Bentley's never out of work, so he might be a problem."

"He said he'd definitely make himself available for this. It came up at the read-through yesterday."

"Oh, well, it should be all right, then. He's the one who's likely to be difficult. I can't think anyone else is going to have much coming up."

Charles cleared his throat. Then he cleared his throat again.

"What's up, Charles? Touch of the old laryngitis?"

"No, Maurice" came the dignified reply. "But . . . isn't there something you've forgotten?"

"What's that? Not your birthday, is it?"

"No."

"Wedding anniversary? But I thought since you and Frances weren't living together anymore, you didn't—"

"No, Maurice. Just think. W.E.T. rang you to check my availability?"

"Yes."

"Well, isn't there something you haven't done?"

The agent was still at a loss. "What's that, then?"

"Come on, Maurice. You haven't checked my bloody availability, have you!"

"What—you mean, I haven't asked whether you'll be free for a fortnight at the end of this contract?"

"Exactly."

There was a silence from the other end of the phone. Then it was interrupted by a sound that could have been an asthmatic having an orgasm. Charles recognized that Maurice was laughing.

"Oh, I'm sorry," said the agent when he was sufficiently recovered to speak. "I am so sorry, Charles. Aren't we being grand?" This idea sent him off into another burst of hysterical gasping. "Oh, dear. Oh, dear. All right, Charles. Here we go. Ready?"

"Yes," Charles replied primly.

"Right. Charles Paris, is it possible that you might be available to record an extra episode of the *Stanislas Braid* series for West End Television in the two weeks immediately following the cessation of your current contract with the company?"

"Hang on a minute," said Charles. "I'll check." Then, after a pause during which someone who possessed an engagements diary would have had time to consult it, he returned to the phone. "I think it might be possible. There are one or two things in the air but nothing firmed up yet."

"I see," said Maurice soberly, playing out the game to its conclusion.

"Yes, I think so long as W.E.T. issues their contract pretty sharpish, we should be all right."

"Oh, good, Charles. That is a weight off my mind."

"Mine, too, Maurice," said Charles, and then spoiled the whole effect by giggling. "Good news, though, isn't it?"

"Excellent. How'd the Rhymer girl shape up at the read-through?"

"Great. She's really good. No, I'm afraid the whole show will be immeasurably better without the services of Sippy Stokes."

"Ah, well . . . Incidentally, did you hear about the inquest?"

"What?" Once again Charles was taken aback by the efficiency of his agent's information service.

"Inquest on Sippy Stokes. Yesterday morning."

"No, I haven't heard anything. What happened?"

"Not a lot. Police asked for an adjournment while they made further investigations."

"Oh."

"Well, you know what that usually means, don't you?"

"What?"

"Means the police think the death's suspicious, doesn't it?"

"Oh," said Charles. "Does it?"

He thought he might need a few drinks at lunchtime to get him through his encounter with the Railton sisters, but he drank whiskey rather than beer. There was a danger that two or three pints diluted with tea would keep him running back and forth to the lavatory all afternoon.

As it did for most people living in central London, the thought of a journey all the way out to Ham Common took on the dimensions of a search for the source of the Nile. That people commuted daily from that kind of distance (it took about half an hour by car) was a constant source of amazement to him.

He caught the tube to Waterloo and got a train to Richmond. From there he took a cab to the address W. T. Wintergreen had given him at the read-through. (What is all this with cabs, Charles Paris? he found himself wondering. Honestly, one three-month contract with W.E.T. and you start behaving like a bloody plutocrat.)

Because of the Nilotic proportions of his imagined expedition, he had left far too much time for the journey, and it was only a quarter to three when he approached his destination. Hastily, so that his early arrival would not be an embarrassment, he managed to stop the cab just before it turned off to Ham Common and spent three-quarters of an hour walking away from the Railtons' cottage toward Ham Gate of Richmond Park.

It was a pleasant April afternoon, and Charles Paris felt as if he were in the depths of the country. Amazing to think all this lay such a comparatively short distance from central London. He really ought to get out more. There were any number of lovely places he could get to without great effort. And being out in the open air must be better than just mooching around his bed-sitter or spending too long in the pub.

But even as he formed these pious intentions, he knew that he would never put them into practice. Like moving out of Hereford Road, organized expeditions into the countryside somehow weren't Charles Paris.

There was an ancient black Volkswagen Beetle parked outside the cottage on whose door Charles knocked at precisely three-thirty. W. T. Wintergreen admitted him with old-fashioned formality.

The cottage that Winifred and Louisa Railton shared was so small it felt like a doll's house, and entering it was like stepping back thirty years. The decor, the furniture, everything about the place had a fifties feel to it.

So did the spread laid out on the table in the tiny sitting room. Charles didn't realize that people still had "tea" on that kind of scale. It was a meal that had never particularly appealed to him, but he couldn't help being impressed by the serried ranks of sandwiches, the plates of rock buns and almond slices on doilies, the—yes, they really were *fairy cakes* (goodness, when had he last seen a fairy cake?), the sugar-dusted Victoria sponge, the ginger cake, the meringues, the Dundee cake. It had an air of excess about it, as if a television designer had been determined to show every aspect of his research into the period and piled on too much detail.

Yet the two Railton sisters seemed to find nothing unusual about the scene. It did not appear that they had pushed the boat out particularly in Charles's honor. The feeling was that they had a tea like this every afternoon of their lives.

And why not? Everything about the cottage bespoke an orderliness, a life of neat predictability, in which untidy emotions were controlled by an unshakable daily timetable. In a television studio or in the St. John Chrysostom Mission for Vagrants Lesser Hall, the Railtons looked anachronistically out of place, whereas in their own environment they fitted in. But then, of course, it was a deeply old-fashioned environment.

Charles looked at the sisters while Winifred went through an elaborate tea-pouring ritual of jugs and strainers and sugar tongs and spoons and tried to estimate how old they were. Louisa was clearly the younger, perhaps by as much as seven years, though it was difficult to tell with women of their age.

Both had salt-and-pepper hair cut in straight lines across the napes of their necks and clipped back with slides on either sides of their heads. Their skins were freckled, but with sun spots rather than the blotches of age. They were thin, both above average height, with Winifred a couple of inches taller than her sister. Winifred wore glasses with almost transparent frames. Both had on flowered print dresses that buttoned all the way up the front and stout buckled sandals at the end of bare, thin freckled legs.

They could really have been any age between sixty and eighty. Charles tried to work it out. If the first W. T.

Wintergreen books had come out before the Second World War, even given exceptional literary precocity Winifred must have been at least twenty in 1935. Which would put her in her late seventies. With Louisa around the seventy mark. Yes, that'd be about right.

The thought of Winifred's books reminded him of the message he had to pass on.

"My wife is a great admirer of your detective stories, er . . ." Like Ben Docherty, he had difficulty in knowing how to address the writer. He settled on ". . . Miss Railton."

She didn't offer any informality of the "Please call me Winifred" variety but simply acknowledged the compliment. "That's very nice to hear, Mr. Paris. I don't think any writer can tire of hearing that people enjoy his or her books. Not, I hasten to add, that it's something which I hear often enough to be in any danger of tiring of it."

"Oh, I'm sure . . ." Charles shrugged ineffectually.

"I was not actually aware that you were married, Mr. Paris."

"Well, I . . ."

"No, I'm sorry. Something someone said around the television company led me to suppose that you were not married."

"I am . . . sort of . . . technically married."

"Ah."

"But we don't live together all of the time."

Any of the time, actually, he thought with a sudden access of misery. He really must ring Frances. See if there was any chance of their getting back together. Yes, he'd make that his number-one priority. Ring her that evening.

"No, my wife was saying," he moved on, "that your books really got her through her adolescence."

"How nice."

"She said the first ones came out in the late thirties."

"Yes. *The Spanish Rapier Murder* was published in 1937." Winifred Railton flashed a modest smile. "I did begin rather young."

"And then you continued till—when, the late fifties, was it?"

"Yes, excepting the war years. Sixteen titles in all."

"Very impressive. Why did you stop? Was it that styles were changing in crime fiction?"

"No, not really." She cleared her throat. "We had domestic problems. Our father was ill. I found I had my time cut out looking after him."

"That's our father," Louisa Railton said suddenly.

She pointed to a framed photograph on the mantelpiece. The clothes dated it as having been taken in the late twenties. A large fair-haired man sat at a garden table. Behind him, with an arm around his shoulder, stood a tall, bespectacled girl in a tennis dress. On his knee sat a smaller girl without glasses who looked up adoringly into her father's eyes. Both children were strikingly pretty, and there was no doubt that they were the originals of the two old women with whom Charles sat over that lavish tea in Ham Common.

The house in front of which the group had been photographed was a huge Edwardian pile. Clearly, though a cottage in Ham Common was a very desirable property, the Railton sisters had come down in the world since their childhood.

Louisa Railton was looking at him with such naked

appeal in her eyes that Charles felt he had to make some comment on the photograph. "A very fine looking man," he said.

"Oh, yes," Louisa agreed.

Winifred seemed unwilling to get sidetracked into a conversation about her late father. "Mr. Paris, you may have wondered why we invited you here this afternoon."

"The thought did cross my mind, yes."

"The fact is, Mr. Paris, we are not at all happy with certain aspects of the way West End Television is making the *Stanislas Braid* series."

"No. Well, I'm afraid television is a difficult medium. I mean, often it's hard for a writer of a book to see why certain changes have been made to a—"

Winifred Railton cut through his flannel. "The fact is, Mr. Paris, that the W. T. Wintergreen books are very dear to us."

"I'm sure they are."

"We have lived through the creation of each and every word of those books."

"I can understand how—"

"Have you ever done any creative writing, Mr. Paris?"

"Yes, I have. I've written a few plays. Never quite had the nerve or the energy to tackle a novel."

"No, but you will know from writing your plays how deeply involved one gets with the characters one creates."

"Certainly."

"And how distressing it is to see one's characters incorrectly portrayed."

"I'm sure it is, Miss Railton. I think, with television, what you have to do is just take the money and forget about it."

"That seems an extremely spineless approach, Mr. Paris."

"Maybe, but it's one that will save you a great deal of heartache. Television is a medium notorious for making changes. Goodness, you should get Will Parton on the subject of things that've been done to his scripts over the years. You wouldn't believe it."

"I don't think Mr. Parton's experiences are really relevant, Mr. Paris. It is not as if he is a creator of characters; he is merely a journeyman, an interpreter of other people's original work."

"I think you may be rather underestimating the skill that he brings to what he does."

"Mr. Paris, he clearly doesn't care about it. He sees his work on the *Stanislas Braid* series as just another job of work."

"Well, yes, but—"

"Do you know, before he started adapting them, he had not even read one of the W. T. Wintergreen books?"

Charles found it interesting to note how Winifred constantly used the pronoun "we" when describing the writing of the books and yet could speak of "the W. T. Wintergreen books" as if they were somehow detached from her.

She allowed a pause for him to appreciate the full enormity of Will Parton's ignorance, and Charles had a horrible fear that he was about to be asked how many of the books *he* had read.

But the danger passed. "As I say, Mr. Paris, there are far too many things in the production which the West End Television people have got completely wrong."

"Yes, I am sure there are a few details that—"

"We are not talking about *details*, Mr. Paris. We are talking about major points in the tone of voice and the characterization in the books which have been wantonly altered."

"Ah." There seemed little point in making further attempts to describe how television worked; better just to sit out their objections and mutter occasional condolences. They had dragged him out all this way just to have a moan, and a moan they were going to have, whether he liked it or not.

"For a start," Winifred Railton began her catalog, "they have got the character of Stanislas Braid completely wrong."

Charles said nothing.

"He is meant to be an intellectual, and yet it is clear that that actor, Russell Whateveritis . . ."

"Bentley."

". . . Russell Bentley has probably never read a book in his life."

"Miss Railton, the whole point about acting is that actors *take on* characters. Just as you don't have to be a murderer to play the part of a murderer, so you don't have to be an intellectual to play the part of an intellectual. You act. You become another personality. You think yourself into the way that personality would react and behave."

"That Russell Bentley doesn't. He makes no effort to think himself into anything. He is exactly the same when he's playing the part as when he's not."

This observation was so unanswerably true that Charles could think of no response to it.

"What's more," Louisa Railton suddenly burst out,

"that actor's got dark brown hair, and anyone who's read even a couple of pages of any of the W. T. Wintergreen books knows that Stanislas Braid didn't have dark brown hair!"

There was a childlike petulance in the outburst, and when her sister calmed her, Charles realized that Winifred did treat Louisa almost like a child. She was protective, overprotective, as if she wanted to keep from her younger sister the truth of what the world was really like.

"While one regrets," Winifred conceded, "that the physical appearance of the characters is wrong, that worries me less than the fact that their *souls* are wrong."

"Their souls?" Charles echoed weakly. He sneaked a look at his watch. Dear God, it was only twenty past four. He'd asked the cab to pick him up at five-thirty, reckoning that two hours was probably an appropriately genteel time to spend over tea. The thought of over an hour more of this catalog of complaints was deeply depressing. While he could feel sympathy with the Railton sisters' objections, he knew that there was nothing he could do to help them. They had been involved with the characters of the W. T. Wintergreen books for over fifty years. They knew nothing of the workings of television. There was no level at which his explanations would make any sense to them.

"Yes, their *souls*," Winifred continued. "Russell Bentley is nowhere near the soul of Stanislas Braid. And that other young man is hopelessly wrong for Blodd. Blodd is not meant to be a cockney. It is stated quite clearly in all the books that Blodd was brought up in Cornwall."

"Surely that's a relatively minor point?"

"It would be a relatively minor point if the *soul* of the

character were right. But it isn't. No one reading the W. T. Wintergreen books could doubt that Blodd is a lugubrious character—positively melancholic at times. And yet this young man plays him as if he were running a sideshow at a funfair."

"Don't any of the characters seem right to you?" Charles pleaded.

"Well, now, the new girl who started yesterday, she seemed right for Christina."

"Yes," Louisa agreed softly. "The coloring's right, apart from anything else."

"Except, of course, they're destroying everything by not calling her Christina. They've got this dreadful idea about introducing someone called Elvira. I mean, the idea that Stanislas Braid could have *two* favorite daughters is just so ridiculous and incongruous."

"And the idea that he would call one of them Elvira . . ."

". . . almost defies belief," W. T. Wintergreen concluded bitterly.

"Well, I think, Miss Railton, that I can set your mind at rest on that matter." Thank goodness there was at least one detail on which he could bring the two poor old dears comfort. He related the conversation he had had with Maurice Skellern about his availability for an extra fortnight, and they were forced to concede that that was encouraging news.

"But," he concluded, "with regard to the other things W.E.T. is doing, I'm afraid I can't be of much help to you. I can't make them change their policies."

"Oh, no, we know that," said Winifred. "You don't think that was why we invited you down here, do you?"

"Well, I hadn't really thought . . . I don't know . . ."

"We invited you down here," she continued firmly, "to give you some tips on how you should play the part of Sergeant Clump."

"Oh, did you?" said Charles weakly.

"Yes. Now tell us—how do you see the character of Sergeant Clump?"

"Well," he began cautiously, "I'd seen him rather as a not very intelligent village policeman."

"Yes, he *is* a not very intelligent village policeman . . ."

"Oh, good," said Charles with considerable relief.

". . . but there's so much more to him than that. Isn't there, Louisa?"

"Oh, yes, Winifred. So much more."

"I mean, when you get into his *soul* . . ."

"Yes, when you get into his *soul* . . ."

And for the remaining hour of his stay the two Railton sisters proceeded to fill Charles Paris in on the hidden depths of the soul of Sergeant Clump.

It was the most exhausting hour of his life. He greeted the arrival of his cab as if it were a food lorry in a refugee camp.

When he finally got back to Hereford Road, Charles Paris drank two inches of Bell's whiskey and fell fast asleep before he even had time to take his clothes off.

He completely forgot about his intention to ring Frances.

CHAPTER
<u>TEN</u>

Two plainclothes policemen arrived at the St. John Chrysostom Mission for Vagrants to interrupt rehearsals on Wednesday morning. They were making some inquiries into the death of Sippy Stokes, "just checking out," as they put it, "how exactly she met her end." The word *murder* was not mentioned, but its shadow immediately loomed in the minds of everyone present.

The new director was furious at this disruption in his schedule. "I am the director of this show," he kept saying, "and it's my job to see that it gets made."

The policemen were impassively firm; they knew he had a job to do, but they also had a job to do. Could they please talk to the members of the cast and production crew who had been in the studio on the previous Wednesday morning? Grudgingly, the new director gave way, and the relevant members of his team were trooped away to be questioned in the St. John Chrysostom Mission for Vagrants Great Hall.

The police said that they had no reason to believe that the death of Sippy Stokes had been anything other than accidental, but in cases like this they did feel an obligation to find out as much about the background as possible.

Charles wondered what new evidence they had uncovered. As he had many times before in his detective career, he envied the police their research facilities. There's nothing like an encounter with a professional criminal investigation to make an amateur sleuth profoundly aware of his amateur status. Why couldn't Charles Paris have been blessed with a convenient brother-in-law on the force, like Lord Peter Wimsey's Inspector Parker? Even Stanislas Braid was not above picking Sergeant Clump's so-called brains when he needed a little privileged information.

But Charles had no such handy informant. He could only guess the stage of investigation that the police had reached. Perhaps something had come up at the postmortem. Maybe the doctor's bland conviction that all he had to do was find the relevant fallen object to fit the dent in Sippy Stokes's skull had proved inadequate. None of the objects had fitted? They were now looking for a murder weapon? An anonymous letter had been sent to the police announcing that Sippy had been murdered? Charles could only conjecture.

The policemen didn't give the impression that their inquiry was particularly urgent, though. They seemed to be going through the motions rather than conducting a life-or-death investigation. Their manner was that of men who had been given a directive from above to make

certain inquiries; they were doing as they were told but
didn't have much faith in the value of what they were
doing. Whether that was actually the case, or whether
their apparent diffidence masked an uncompromising de-
termination to get at the truth, was another question at
whose answer Charles could only guess.

They asked the assembled crowd of actors and production staff what they had been doing between eleven and
twelve the previous Wednesday morning, and all the
answers conformed with what Charles had witnessed in
the canteen and Studio A during that period.

All the answers except one. Tony Rees, the quiet
A.S.M. who seemed content to live in the shadow of the
more flamboyant Mort Verdon, produced a different version of events from what Charles remembered.

"I went to the canteen for coffee as soon as the break
was called," the young man told the police. His voice
was so rarely heard that it was quite a shock to hear how
thick the Welsh accent was. "Then I was going back to
the studio when I remembered I had to pick up a props
list from Design Department. So I went up there."

"And what time did you get back into Studio A?"

"I don't remember exactly."

"Well, was it before twelve o'clock or after?"

"Definitely after," said Tony Rees.

The police did not question this answer, but Charles
Paris knew it was a lie. He clearly remembered seeing
the A.S.M. behind the set at about a quarter to twelve,
only moments before his unpleasant discovery in the
props room.

He also remembered that at the moment Tony Rees had
looked extremely guilty.

* * *

Immediately on his return from the St. John Chrysostom Mission for Vagrants Great Hall to the St. John Chrysostom Mission for Vagrants Lesser Hall, Charles was swept up into rehearsal by the new director. ("I'm the director of this show, and already far too much of my time has been wasted this morning.") And when he next had a break, Charles noticed with dismay that Tony Rees had left the rehearsal room.

The following day he wasn't there, either. According to Mort Verdon, the A.S.M. was laid up with the flu. So Charles couldn't pursue his most intriguing line of investigation.

In fact, the only constructive thing he did the rest of that week was to pluck up courage and ring Frances. She agreed to have dinner with him on Saturday night. She didn't sound over the moon about the idea, but at least she agreed.

"Dear, oh, dear, Charles Paris, are you becoming a theatrical smoothie?"

"Hardly, Frances."

"Well, I mean, taking me out to dinner at Joe Allen's." She looked around the dark wood-paneled basement, with its long noisy bar, its red checked tablecloths, its blackboard menus, its swooping waiters in long white aprons.

"Oh, come on. We're only here because the food's good. And it's cheap."

"Nothing to do with the fact that it's a favored haunt of stars of stage and television?"

"No, of course not. I'm not like that."

"No?"

"No. Anyway, they didn't give us a table along the wall where they put all the stars."

"They didn't, did they, the rotters? Perhaps you have a little way to go before you're really a big telly name."

"Shut up, Frances."

"But it's true, Charles. You are different. Subtly different. Being in lucrative employment has wrought a mysterious change in you."

"No, it hasn't."

"You wouldn't have taken me to Joe Allen's a year or so ago. You'd have made some disparaging remark about theatrical trendies if the place had even been mentioned. Now you think it's just possible that you might be becoming a theatrical trendy."

"No, I don't." But the idea she had planted did, for the first time in his life, have a little sneaking appeal. Why, after all, shouldn't he be successful? He'd waited long enough, in all conscience. He'd served his time. Why shouldn't Charles Paris become famous in his declining years?

And if he could be a success in his professional life, why couldn't he get his private life sorted out, too? Time for decisive action.

"Frances . . ." he began.

"Yes?"

"I wanted just to talk for a moment about us."

"Us? That sounds ominous."

"Where we stand."

"We're sitting down," she said, evasively flippant.

"No, I meant—"

"I know what you meant, Charles. All right." She laid

her hands, almost as if she were laying her cards, on the red-and-white-checked tablecloth in front of her. "Where do we *stand*? Well, my *stance* is that of a headmistress of a girls' school, living in a flat in Highgate. Your *stance* is that of an intermittently employed actor living in a bed-sitter I'd rather not think about in Bayswater. My job is extremely time-consuming and uses up most of my energy. Your job is intermittently time-consuming, and I don't think I really want to know how you use up the rest of your energy. We are neither of us in the first flush of youth." She lifted her hands up in a "That's about it" gesture. "Yes, Charles, I'd say that's where we *stand*."

"You have forgotten to mention one thing, Frances."

"Really? What's that?"

"That we're married to each other."

"Oh, Charles, I wouldn't put it as strongly as that."

"How strongly would you put it, then?"

"Well, I think I'd go as far as to say that we're not divorced."

"Oh, thank you."

She wasn't making it easy for him. On the other hand, why should she? There was too much history between them. Too many promising starts at repairing their relationship had come unstuck for her to be anything other than wary in her dealings with her husband.

"Am I to gather that this is another attempt at a *rapprochement*, Charles?"

"Yes. Yes, Frances, it is."

"I see. And how far are you proposing to *rapproche* this time?"

"As far as possible."

"All the way? I say. Dramatic stuff. Do you mean you want to *rapproche* your way back into my bed?"

"No. Well, yes, I do. But not just that."

"What, you mean *rapproche* your way back into living together? Even *rapproche* your way back into"—her voice dropped to an awestruck whisper—"being *married* to each other?"

He nodded. "That's what I mean." She looked bewildered. "What do you say?"

"What do I say?" She mused for a moment, as if considering a plethora of possibilities. "Well, I think the first thing I'd say is Why?"

"Why?"

"Yes, *why* should we go back to being married? It didn't work the first time."

"No, I agree. But if we tried harder—"

"I tried extremely hard the first time, Charles," she said with some asperity.

"All right. If *I* tried harder."

"I have seen a few of your attempts at trying harder. Not always very impressive. No, I don't think that's a very good argument as to *why* we should get back together."

"But, Frances, I'm not getting any younger."

"And that is an even worse argument. You are offering me the unique opportunity of sharing your arthritis and incontinence, are you?"

"No, I'm just saying that, I don't know, we do have a lot of things in common."

"Name one."

"Well . . ." The pause was longer than it should have been. "Juliet."

"Yes, we have a daughter in common, but she is now grown up, with a family of her own. We no longer need to 'stay together for the sake of the children,' particularly since we didn't stay together at the time when that argument might have been relevant."

No, she certainly wasn't making it easy. He tried another, more sentimental tack. "Even after all this time, Frances, and after everything that's happened, still, even now, in a strange way, we were made for each other."

"I blame the manufacturer," said Frances.

"But it's true. We do still love each other."

She was silent. She looked away from him. When she looked back, her eyes were glazed with unshed tears. "Yes"—she sighed—"it's true. But it's not relevant."

"Of course it's relevant. If two people love each other—"

"Then what? It doesn't mean they can live together. Good God, Charles, we're living proof that it doesn't mean that."

"Love is important."

"I don't deny it. But a lot of other things are important, too. And though I don't question the quality of your love, I have less faith in your ability to deal with the other things in life."

"Well . . ."

"Come on, you have absolutely no interest in domesticity. And by domesticity I don't mean housework or anything like that. I just mean living in a house with someone else."

"No, but . . ."

"You can't deny it, can you, Charles?"

"No." He sighed and gazed into the middle distance.

"There are some things I'm interested in, though. Even good at. I often think if life were all making love and getting drunk, I could cope with it better."

"Yes, I think most of us could. But I'm afraid it isn't. And even if it were, some people could be forgiven for wishing that the lovemaking was always directed towards the same person."

The bitterness of her final words reminded him of how much he had hurt her in the past. At that moment he felt infinite regret for his behavior toward her. At that moment he vowed he would never again make love to any woman other than Frances. At that moment he vowed that if Frances wouldn't have him, he would never make love to anyone ever again. At that moment . . .

"Hmm. Well, Frances, it sounds as if you don't really want to *rapproche* that far."

"No."

"So won't we see each other again?"

She let out a huge exasperated sigh of frustration. "Yes, of course we'll bloody see each other again, Charles Paris! God, I know you're an actor, but why do you have to make everything so dramatic all the time? Like it or not—and most of the time I don't think I do like it—we are involved with each other. I can't just shake you off and pretend you don't exist—much as I would often like to. No, you're part of me. I've *got* Charles Paris in the same way that some people have *got* color blindness . . . or hay fever . . . or eczema."

Charles grinned. "Do you know, Frances, I think that was a compliment."

She grinned, too. Unwillingly. "Nearest you're going

to bloody get to one," she said, and leaned across the table to ruffle his hair.

They had a second bottle of wine and finished the meal in high good spirits. Charles put his arm around his wife as they left the restaurant.

They were just at the door when he caught sight of two familiar figures at a table in the far corner. A man and a woman, heads bowed together, deep in intimate conversation.

The man was Ben Docherty, producer of *Stanislas Braid*. But it was the woman he was with who interested Charles.

She was the Blue Nun. Gwen Rhymer. Mother of Joanne Rhymer.

So maybe Ben Docherty had had a vested interest in the recasting of the part of Christina Braid?

CHAPTER ELEVEN

The filming for the second episode of *Stanislas Braid* was standard W.E.T. filming; in other words, no location was more than half a mile away from W.E.T. House. But the production team did not have the freedom of selection that some other series enjoyed. *Stanislas Braid* was set in the thirties—or at least in that cloud-cuckoo Golden-Age-of-Detective-Fiction Country-House-Murder time that approximates the thirties—and so the usual moody shots of urban decay at the tail-end of the twentieth century could not be indulged.

As a result, the location managers had their work cut out finding suitable venues for the Great Detective's investigations. It wasn't that there weren't plenty of buildings of the right period—London is full of them—but tracking down buildings unmarred by television aerials, entryphones, or an adjacent McDonald's was not so easy. Double yellow lines had to be painted out, parking meters disguised as lampposts, and glass-sided telephone boxes dressed up as red ones. There were many interruptions to the schedule as traffic of far too contemporary a design was diverted and the five expensively hired vintage vehicles were repositioned to give an illusion of metropolitan bustle.

(The authentic 1930s bus had cost so much to hire that Ben Docherty insisted it should earn its keep by appearing in almost every shot. Its destination board was constantly changed to give the impression that the whole bus network of London was on the screen.)

Anachronistic passersby also had to be kept out of shot, and as filming always attracts crowds—particularly when the setting is historical—this was a major problem. The limited number of background artistes that Ben Docherty's budget allowed stood around in their thirties garb as city gents, ladies of leisure, policemen, barrow boys, nurses, newspaper boys, and flower sellers (it is an unalterable rule of British television that any London daytime exterior set before the war shall include at least one newspaper boy and one flower seller), but there was always the threat of the irruption of a track-suited jogger, a leather-clad motorbike messenger, or a wandering Rastafarian with a ghetto blaster. The location managers were kept busy fielding such invasions.

The result of all these restrictions was that the shooting tended to be very intimate—a lot of close-ups against authentically ancient backgrounds. Opening the shots out always ran the risk of including glimpses of an Indian takeaway, a distant billboard advertising computers, or an errant punk listening to a Walkman.

These difficulties added to the problems of a schedule that was already tight. *Stanislas Braid* was being made on a fortnightly turnaround—a week's rehearsal, two days' filming, three days in the studio, to produce fifty-two minutes of television—so there wasn't much room for finesse in the production. The new director, who, needless to say, saw himself as the latest messiah of the British film industry, was constantly frustrated in his attempts to "make every frame a Rembrandt" by Ben Docherty's urgings that they were slipping behind schedule. The producer was terrified of losing time so early in the production. Most of the later episodes involved filming outside London, and what with the amount of traveling and local difficulties likely to be encountered, the threat of slippage would be much greater then.

Charles Paris did not have a great deal to do in that week's filming. Sergeant Clump was rarely off his home patch of Little Breckington, so his involvement in the London scenes was limited. This gave Charles plenty of opportunity to observe the other people around the set and, particularly, to think about the death of Sippy Stokes.

Most of the potential suspects were there. Jimmy Sheet, to whose shaky marriage an indiscreet Sippy Stokes might have posed a threat, acted his scenes efficiently and spent a lot of time signing autographs for the crowds that gathered.

Russell Bentley, when not showing resentment that more people asked for Jimmy Sheet's autograph than for his own, spent most of his time paraphrasing his lines, much to the fury of Will Parton. It also infuriated W. T.

Wintergreen and Louisa Railton, who insisted on watching everything that went on.

Filming offered great opportunities for paraphrase to an actor like Russell Bentley. Since the scenes were mostly done in very short takes, the lines were not really learned, simply mugged up seconds before each take. And if the lighting, the sound, the background action, and the framing of the shot had worked, the director was unlikely to worry about how approximate the lines might have been. So Russell Bentley had wonderful opportunities to say fewer and fewer lines as Stanislas Braid might have said them and more and more as Russell Bentley would say them. None of these opportunities did he waste.

The star seemed to have developed a very good working relationship with his new daughter. Joanne Rhymer, as well as being attractive, really was a very good little actress, and though Russell Bentley kept complaining that the relationship was a bit too good to be true, they played their scenes together well. So her appearance on the set was good news for him.

Presumably, it was also good news for Ben Docherty, since it advanced his campaign with the girl's mother.

But surely neither of them would have resorted to murder to make that good news happen? Would they?

What about the Railtons? What about Will Parton, come to that? They were all better off without Sippy Stokes. But, again, murder seemed an extreme way of defending the integrity of one's writing.

No, there was only one person who Charles thought could help his investigations in any meaningful way.

Tony Rees. And the assistant stage manager was still off work with the flu.

The first studio day of that episode, Wednesday, began with another row between the new director and W. T. Wintergreen. It was about a set that had made its first appearance that day. Christina Braid's bedroom.

"I'm sorry," the crime writer said. "It just shouldn't be like that. It's too bright. The blue is too bright."

"It shouldn't be blue, anyway," her sister contributed. "In the books it's made quite clear that Christina's room is done in the subtlest of pastel shades. Almost white wallpaper, with a tiny motif of a pale yellow flower. And bedclothes of the palest pink."

"I'm sorry," said the new director, "but this is how the designer sees it."

"Well, then, I'm afraid he sees it wrong," W. T. Wintergreen objected calmly. "Has the designer actually read any of the books?"

"I don't know. I expect he read one or two before the series started."

Oh, yes? thought Charles. I bet he didn't.

W. T. Wintergreen was implacable. "It's wrong. It'll have to be changed."

"It will not be changed," said the new director. "It has just been built, and we have a very busy schedule for the next three days. There is no way it could be changed even if anyone wanted it changed."

"I want it changed," said W. T. Wintergreen.

"So do I," Louisa Railton agreed.

"Well, you can both forget it. Look, I am the director

of this show, and it's my job to see that the show gets made. And if you keep wasting my time, it won't be.''

''I am not wasting your time. I am merely trying to get things right.''

''Listen, if you two continue to disrupt my production, I will have you banned from the studio.''

''You can't do that. I am W. T. Wintergreen. I wrote the books.''

''And I am the director, and I am making a television program! Or trying to!''

The argument was clearly going to run for some little while yet. Charles Paris drifted over to the set of Stanislas Braid's study. There was no one about. He moved toward the mantelpiece and picked up the candlestick that had been missing at the time of Sippy Stokes's death.

He lifted it up and turned it over. He didn't quite know what he was expecting—dried blood, a lingering dark hair?—but whatever it was, he was disappointed. Just the discolored base of a brass candlestick with the name of the hire firm painted on it in blue.

He put it back. Then he remembered that the set had been completely dismantled and rebuilt during the last fortnight. It was quite possible that the candlesticks had been put back the other way around.

With a burst of excitement, he picked up the second candlestick and upturned it.

Nothing except the name of the hire company. Or at least nothing the naked eye could discern. Maybe a police forensic examination could find some minuscule traces for incrimination. Once again he wondered what the police were up to. Had they written off the death as an accident? Or was their investigation still proceeding?

"What are you doing?"

Charles turned at the voice to face Mort Verdon. The stage manager was looking at him suspiciously.

"Just interested in where these things were hired from."

"Uh-huh." Mort didn't sound convinced. "Sorry, we have to be careful. You'd be amazed how much stuff disappears off television studio sets."

"Really?"

"Oh, yes, boofle. Lots of light-fingered people about, you know. Whenever it's something historical, when you've got a few antiques littered round the place, you'd be surprised how little of it finds its way back to the hire companies. There's a great deal of, what shall we say, natural wastage?"

"Oh, well, Mort, I can assure you that I wouldn't dream of—"

"No, never really thought you would, boofle. Just . . . as I say, we have to keep an eye on things."

"Of course."

"Series like this is an absolute field day for those of kleptomaniac tendencies. All this stuff . . ."

"Yes. Has a lot gone missing already?"

"Oh, yes. Those candlesticks, for a start."

"What do you mean?"

"Those aren't the ones we had on the first episode."

"Really?"

"No. The first pair . . . disappeared at the end of the week."

"Where do you think they went?"

The stage manager shrugged. "Some member of the production team sneaked them out under his anorak, I suppose. Expect they're on a stall in Church Street Market by now. We had to hire some more.''

''Oh.''

''Never mind. W.E.T. can afford it.''

''Ben Docherty keeps saying the budget's very tight on this show.''

''The budget may be tight, but W.E.T. can still afford it.'' Mort Verdon's wry smile suggested that, like Russell Bentley, he hadn't much time for commercial television companies pleading poverty.

''Hmm. Well, look, Mort, I'm sorry you suspected that I—''

''No, I didn't, really. Not when I saw it was you. Anyway, actors very rarely walk off with things from the set.''

''Oh, good. I'm glad that my profession has a reputation for honesty.''

''No, actors usually walk off with their costumes.''

''Ah.''

''Be surprised at the end of a series how many leather jackets and tailor-made suits somehow don't find their way back to Wardrobe.''

''Well, Mort, I really don't think you have to worry about that happening with me on *Stanislas Braid*, do you?''

The stage manager looked appraisingly at Sergeant Clump's ancient blue serge and grinned. ''No, Charles, I think we'll be all right there.'' A thought struck him. ''Unless of course you're one of those fetishists who gets his kicks in bed from dressing up as a policeman.''

''Oh, no!'' Charles's face took on a horrified expression. ''Mort, how on earth did you find out?''

* * *

The break for lunch was announced, and Charles was about to make another bid for a Personal Best to the bar when he noticed Tony Rees.

The assistant stage manager might well have been around the studio all morning, but Charles hadn't seen him. He looked pale and wretched, so the flu that had laid him low for a week appeared to have been genuine. But what interested Charles more was that Tony Rees also looked furtive. He was hanging around the fringes of the set as if waiting for all the rest of the production team to leave.

Charles decided that he, too, would linger. He wanted to talk to the A.S.M., but first he wanted to see what the young man was up to. Charles called a loud "See you later" to no one in particular and then made for the props-room exit. He opened the double doors and let them close with a soft thump, like an intake of breath. He remained inside the studio and moved to a vantage point behind the window of Christina Braid's bedroom. Gauzy print curtains ("far too strident" in W. T. Wintergreen's estimation) hid him from the rest of the studio but did not impede his view of Tony Rees.

The A.S.M. stood immobile for a long couple of minutes, testing the silence of the studio. It was complete; after the bustle of the morning, the stillness was absolute.

Satisfied that he was alone, he moved briskly into action and started straight toward the bedroom set. Charles pushed himself back into the angle between two flats but realized with horror that Tony Rees was coming around the edge of the set toward him. The actor dropped to an uncomfortable crouch behind a loudspeaker.

Tony Rees was too preoccupied to be vigilant. Having made the decision that he was alone, he had no suspicions of surveillance. He walked quickly past Charles, who was close enough to have touched his trouser leg, and continued around the back of the set.

But only ten or fifteen yards farther on he stopped. There was a sound of something being moved, fabric at first, then maybe metal. Charles wished he could see what was going on. He craned around as far as he dared from his uncomfortable crouch but still couldn't see enough. He leaned forward on all fours.

This was a foolish position for someone dressed as Sergeant Clump to take up. One of the features of the sergeant in the W. T. Wintergreen books—and one of the few that had been carried over into the television series—was that he always had in his breast pocket a row of pencils with which to scribble laboriously in a notebook his criminal theories (all of them doomed to be proved wrong by the quicksilver intellect of Stanislas Braid).

Now it is a simple fact of gravity that pencils do not stay in the breast pocket of someone leaning forward on all fours, and sure enough, a cascade of them fell to the floor in front of Charles.

The sounds around the back of the set ceased instantly. Charles, scrabbling to pick up his pencils, saw Tony Rees's feet appear in front of him. Using the innocent expression that had got him such a big laugh in *See How They Run* in Chester ("about as funny as being woken up in the middle of the night by a motorbike"—*Liverpool Daily Post*), he said, "I seem to have dropped my pencils."

"Oh?" said Tony Rees, and he stood unmoving in front of the prostrate policeman.

Charles gathered together the last of the pencils and stood up. "That's all of them," he said fatuously.

"Yes," said Tony Rees, still immobile.

"Well, I was just about to leave the studio," Charles babbled on.

"So was I," said Tony Rees.

They walked out silently, side by side. Whatever it was the A.S.M. had been doing around the back of the set, he had no intention of continuing it now that he knew he had been observed. Equally, he did not intend to leave Charles alone in the studio to check on his activities.

"I wondered if we could talk?" said Charles diffidently as they walked up toward the bar.

"I'm busy this lunch hour," said Tony Rees, sullenly Welsh.

"Well, maybe some other time?"

"Maybe."

Whatever the nature of Tony Rees's "busyness," it seemed to take second place to keeping an eye on Charles. As he commiserated with Will Parton in the bar over the latest sequence of rewrites Ben Docherty and Dilly Muirfield had demanded, Charles was aware of the A.S.M. sitting alone at a table in the corner, making one Perrier last a long time. And when Charles and Will decided to nip down to canteen for a W.E.T.-subsidized steak, Tony Rees coincidentally also decided that it was time he had something to eat.

Whatever the secret he kept behind the set was, the A.S.M. didn't want Charles to sneak into the studio and investigate it.

* * *

Charles Paris was kept busy at the beginning of the afternoon with another Little Breckington Police Station scene. Though this involved three policemen from other forces, Charles did not recognize any of the background artistes involved. He felt a momentary pang for the dashed hopes of the two who had seen *Stanislas Braid* as a prospect of long-term employment.

The scene involved, as usual, Sergeant Clump putting forward his thesis about the solution of the current crime, which this week was "The Italian Stiletto Murder," and Stanislas Braid, with a few deft thrusts of logic, cutting it to shreds. All of these scenes were so similar that Charles envisaged problems with lines before the end of the series; even after two recordings, he was worried about which speeches fitted in which episode.

And Russell Bentley, whose skill with paraphrase during the filming seemed to have gone to his head, now regarded every line as merely an idea around which he could embroider. This led to conflicts with the new director, who insisted, "I'm the director of this show, and I have to hear the lines as printed if I'm going to know when to cut my shots." It also made life difficult for Charles, since he never knew when his cue had come. The only indication he received was a quizzical silence coupled with a mildly reproachful look from Russell Bentley.

But these were mere ripples compared to Studio A's major storm of the afternoon, which occurred in a scene involving Stanislas Braid, his daughter, Christina, and Sergeant Clump. The action was simple enough. Because of the danger of the mission he was about to undertake,

Stanislas entrusted his precious daughter to the care of the trustworthy British bobby. Rehearsal for the scene the week before had been slightly sticky, because Russell Bentley kept objecting to the extravagant terms in which Stanislas Braid referred to his daughter.

"I mean, it is over the top, love," he said at one point to the new director, whose name he never attempted to master. "You know, okay, they love each other as father and daughter should, but lines like 'I want this, my most precious jewel, kept in the strongest casket in Christendom' sound a bit much to me. I mean, can't he just say, 'She means a lot to me. I want you to guard her with your life, Clump'? Something along those lines'd be better, wouldn't you agree, er, old man?" He appealed to Charles, of whose name he remained equally ignorant.

The discussions had rumbled on through rehearsal without any final decisions being made about changing the lines. Charles thought Russell Bentley had a good point, for once. The Stanislas/Christina relationship was potentially cloying, and though the casting of Joanne Rhymer made the lines possible, they did still seem excessive. Will Parton also thought the relationship was a bit much, but he was pleased with the way he had adapted it from the books and reckoned he had "taken the curse off it" sufficiently.

So he didn't want changes to his carefully wrought dialogue. And, needless to say, W. T. Wintergreen and Louisa wanted the relationship more sugary rather than less. As usual, they couldn't understand why a single word had been changed from the original book.

The new director didn't seem too concerned about the issue. Like all directors, he regarded words as just things that got in the way of his pictures. But because it was easier for him to work from a fixed text than one that kept changing, he recommended leaving the lines as they were.

When they rehearsed the scene that afternoon in the studio, Russell Bentley spoke his speeches more or less as written. "Sergeant Clump, I am handing into your care a jewel of inestimable price. She is the star who from her birth has shone over my life."

"Nice bit of twinkling," Charles murmured to Joanne Rhymer when they broke after this line.

She grinned at him, a rather intimate grin. She looked very like her notorious mother when she did that. Charles felt a little illicit flicker of interest.

When they came to shoot the scene, however, Russell Bentley, as he so often did, produced completely different lines. "Sergeant Clump," he said, "my daughter's a good kid. You look after her properly, or I'll have your guts for garters."

Remarkably, at the end of the short recording, the floor manager said, "That was fine. Okay, just wait for a 'clear' on it and we'll move on."

So the change of lines couldn't have affected the new director's camera angles. Probably so busy watching the pictures that he hadn't even heard what was said.

But before the floor manager had time to move them on to the next scene, the studio was suddenly invaded.

"Stop! Stop!" shouted an elderly but authoritative voice.

It was W. T. Wintergreen, sailing magnificently in with Louisa in tow, determined to save her dialogue.

"We've got to go on," said the floor manager gently.

"No! We will not go on until that last scene has been done right!"

The floor manager was silent for a moment, receiving instructions in his earpiece. No doubt having filtered out the obscenities, he announced diplomatically, "The director says he's the director of the show and we've got to get on with the next scene."

"I am the writer of the W. T. Wintergreen books, and I say we don't go on until we get it right. I will not have actors massacring my characters."

"Hardly massacring the characters, old girl," protested Russell Bentley, as oblivious of W. T. Wintergreen's name as he was of anyone else's. "Just making the characters a bit more realistic."

"I wrote them realistically."

"Yes, they are completely real!" Louisa chipped in.

"Well, I'm afraid the kind of reality people expect nowadays is a bit different. Listen, I have a reputation in television. If the public see that a show's got Russell Bentley in it, then they—"

The star's thousandth reiteration of this routine was surprisingly interrupted. By Ben Docherty. And, even more remarkably, by Ben Docherty being decisive.

He burst into the studio like a whirlwind. No doubt he was well fueled by his lunch, but whatever its cause, his performance was impressive.

"Right," he roared. "That's enough!"

The entire studio was silent.

"We've wasted quite enough time on this sort of discussion! We're slipping behind schedule, and we can't risk doing that. Miss Wintergreen, the directors and I have been very patient. We have listened to your suggestions and followed many of them. But now I'm afraid you are just becoming disruptive. I must ask you and your sister to leave the studio and to keep away from W.E.T. premises until the production of *Stanislas Braid* is finished!''

''What?''

''You heard what I said.''

''But I wrote the books. I created Stanislas Braid.''

''That is neither here nor there. You must leave!''

W. T. Wintergreen stood her ground, preparing to defend herself. But then Louisa Railton began to cry, weakly, feebly, like a child. Winifred put her arm around her sister's shoulder and said quietly, ''Very well.''

''Tony.'' Ben Docherty summoned the assistant stage manager. ''Will you please escort Miss Wintergreen and her sister out of the building.''

Tony did as he was told. The three of them, a small funeral cortege, trooped out of Studio A in total silence.

Charles realized it was his chance. He was not needed in the next scene. He moved surreptitiously to the edge of the set, then slipped behind, just as he had seen Tony Rees do earlier in the day.

There was no one in sight, no one to interfere with this search. He gauged how far along Tony had gone and dropped to his knees.

At the bottom of the flats there was a roll of excess canvas. Charles probed along its length, feeling for some unexpected shape.

He found it. Through the canvas it felt thin, hard, and metallic.

He unwound it from its hiding place.

It was an Italian stiletto. The point felt wickedly sharp.

He thought back a fortnight. Once again he saw Tony Rees rising guiltily from something he had hidden at this very spot.

While they were recording "The Brass Candlestick Murder," Sippy Stokes had been killed with a candlestick.

Now they were recording "The Italian Stiletto Murder." Who was *its* victim intended to be?

CHAPTER
<u>TWELVE</u>

"Is there another murder on your mind, Charles?"

"Well, there might be, Frances. Why do you ask?"

"You sound preoccupied. You sound like you do when you're investigating a murder. Is it that actress whose death was in the papers a week or so back?"

"Mm."

"And do you reckon you know who killed her?"

"Yes."

"Then go to the police."

"I haven't got any evidence. In my experience, when I go to the police with no evidence, they laugh at me."

"Yes. Well, one can see their point. Anyway, be careful, Charles."

"The fact that you say that must mean you care, Frances."

"Stop fishing for compliments. Of course I care."

"Good."

"But don't assume that I'm particularly happy about the situation."

"No." A little, prickly silence on the telephone line. "I did mean what I said, Frances. I really would like us to get back together again on a permanent basis."

"Huh. No other women?"

"No other women."

"Suggest it again when you've gone a whole year without making love to any other women and maybe I'll listen more seriously."

"A year from today?"

"Yes. You know you'll never manage it, Charles."

"Of course I will. Easy-peasy."

"We'll see. Is it tomorrow you're off to Dorset?"

"Late afternoon, yes."

"And is your murder suspect going with you?"

"Yes."

"Well, don't do anything stupid."

"You see, you *do* care."

"Don't push your luck, Charles Paris," Frances growled.

Why was it, he reflected, that coach journeys took adults straight back to infantile behavior? As soon as the *Stanislas Braid* team entered the coaches chartered by W.E.T. to take them to Swanage, the silliness began, and it continued all the way to Dorset. Songs, party games, impressions of members of the production team, paper darts, all helped along by the bottle of wine someone had thoughtfully provided. They were weak with laughter by the time they arrived.

He certainly had no chance to talk to Tony Rees. Just

as he had had no chance to talk to Tony Rees for the last week. The A.S.M. avoided him deliberately. For the journey to Dorset, he waited to see which coach Charles got into and deliberately got into the other.

Still . . . "The Italian Stiletto Murder" had been safely recorded, and no real-life murder had marred the proceedings. Charles was beginning to doubt the strength of the chain of logic that had seemed so strong when he had found the hidden weapon. At times he even questioned his conviction that Sippy Stokes had been murdered. Time blurred things. The more days went by and the less new evidence came to light, the lazier his interest grew.

And even if she had been murdered, did it actually matter that much? Everyone was happier for her death. Even Rick Landor, back in charge as director of this episode, seemed restored to his normal good humor.

Charles did not believe in absolutes of right and wrong, the necessity that for every crime there must be a matching retribution. As he traveled down in the coach to Swanage, diverted by the silliness around him, and particularly by the chatter of Joanne Rhymer, he could entertain the possibility of Sippy Stokes's death slipping quietly out of his mind. Never to return.

The W.E.T. contingent arrived in Swanage about five and checked into their various accommodations. Charles was delighted to find that his newfound status as a regular character in a television series entitled him to a room in an AA three-star hotel, along with Russell Bentley, Jimmy Sheet, Will Parton, Joanne Rhymer, and Rick Landor. Other members of the cast were scattered in various two-star hotels. The W.E.T. staff members, following many years' experience in the management of expenses, had mostly opted for hotels cheap enough to ensure that they made a profit on their overnight allowances.

Charles checked into his room, which commanded what would presumably be a good view of Swanage Bay when the weather wasn't so dull. The sky had gotten darker and damper the farther west the coach went, and by the time they arrived in Swanage, everything was shrouded in a thick sea mist. The limited visibility did not augur well for the next two days' filming.

Still, that was Rick Landor and Ben Docherty's problem, not his. At times, the passivity of being an actor almost drove Charles Paris to distraction, but there were also times, like this one, of gleeful irresponsibility in his chosen profession. And, as ever, being in a strange hotel room gave him a lift. It seemed to recharge his identity, give him a feeling of starting afresh, the sensation that nobody had any expectations of him and he could behave in any way he chose.

The way he chose initially was not very different from the way he might have chosen at any other point in his life. He decided to take advantage of his "resident" status and go down to the hotel bar for an out-of-hours drink.

On the way he met Will Parton, in a toweling dressing gown. The writer was going down to the hotel swimming pool. So were most of the others, except for Jimmy Sheet, who was going to work out in the hotel gym. Did Charles fancy joining them?

Well, no, actually. He had swum in his time and quite enjoyed it, but the effort of all that changing and getting wet and getting dry and changing back again always seemed to Charles disproportionate to the amount of pleasure involved. And when the charms of diving into a swimming pool were set against those of diving into a large Bell's . . . well, there was no contest.

He had a couple of large Bell's and, having agreed with the barman in about half a dozen different formulae of words that it was very foggy, decided, since none of the rest of the *Stanislas Braid* team had reappeared, that he would go out for a walk before dinner.

He hadn't bothered to go up to his room for his coat and was surprised at how wet the mist was when he got outside. In fact, rain was driving with some persistence through the murk. By the time Charles had gone a couple of hundred yards down toward the front, he had decided that he must either curtail his walk or risk the final disintegration of his sodden sports jacket, so the sight of a pub was a welcome one. A quick drink, he reckoned, and the rain might have eased off a bit before he went back up the hill to the hotel for dinner.

Inside the pub, the light seemed as murky and steamy as it did outside. A few people stood around in raincoats and anoraks. It was only just after seven, so the pub was not yet very full.

But sitting facing him in an alcove at the far end of the room, Charles saw a figure he recognized: Tony Rees.

On the evidence of the last week, Charles fully expected the A.S.M. to walk straight out of the pub and was amazed to see Tony rising with a half of lager in his hand and coming to intercept him with an expression on his face that could almost be described as genial.

"Charles, good evening. Can I get you a drink?"

"Well, why don't I get you one, Tony?"

Charles made for the bar but was diverted by the A.S.M., who took him firmly by the arm and led him to a seat in the alcove adjacent to the one from which Tony had just risen. "Now, what's it to be?"

"Large Bell's'd be good."

"Fine. Large Bell's it shall be, Charles Paris," said the A.S.M. loudly and bonhomously.

While Tony was at the bar, Charles puzzled over what could have brought on this sudden affability but had reached no conclusions by the time his drink arrived.

Tony Rees sat down opposite him, still with the same half of lager. "Cheers."

"Cheers."

"You said you wanted to talk to me, Charles."

"Yes. Yes, I did." He was again taken aback by the ease with which he was being offered the interview, which had been evaded all week.

"Well, what was it about?"

"Candlesticks . . . for a start."

"Oh," said Tony Rees, and his face fell. "How much do you know?"

"I know that a candlestick was moved off the set of Stanislas Braid's study on the Wednesday of the first episode, just before Sippy Stokes died."

"I see."

"And I know what happened to it subsequently."

"Do you?"

"Yes. You also know what happened to it subsequently, don't you?"

"Well . . ."

"Yes, you do, Tony. You know exactly what happened."

The A.S.M. looked horror-struck. He reached forward

for his drink, but his hand was shaking too much to hold it. The half-pint leaped from his hand onto the table, cannoning its contents out into Charles's lap.

"I'm so terribly sorry." Tony Rees was instantly at his side with a handkerchief, making ineffectual efforts to mop up the mess.

"Don't worry, Tony. Hasn't made me much wetter than I was already." Charles indicated two heavily anoraked figures who were just leaving the pub. "Don't envy anyone who's going back out there at the moment. Come on, let me get you another drink."

It was a pleasure to stand up. The lager-drenched trousers didn't cling to his legs quite so clammily in a vertical position. He bought another half and, since his own drink seemed mysteriously to have emptied itself, another large Bell's.

When he sat down again, he continued in a business-like fashion. "I haven't forgotten what we were talking about."

"No."

"Candlesticks . . . and stilettos."

"Yes. You saw me going to get the stiletto that lunch break when I didn't realize there was anyone in the studio."

Charles nodded.

"Well, what are you proposing to do about it, then?"

"I don't know, Tony. It depends really on how much you are prepared to tell me. Then maybe I suppose we go to the police."

"The police! Over something like that? But everyone does it."

If Tony Rees's speech had sounded flabbergasted, then

Charles's reaction to it sounded even more so. "Everyone does it!"

"Yes."

"What are we talking about, Tony?"

"Nicking stuff from the studio."

"Oh, are we?"

"It's like a perk of the job, Charles. And it's not as if W.E.T. can't afford it," said Tony Rees, echoing Mort Verdon's words.

"So you nick stuff on a regular basis?"

"If you put it like that, yes. Not big stuff. And stuff I know I can get rid of without too much bother."

"Stuff like candlesticks and stilettos?"

"Yes. Got a dealer down Church Street Market I know'll give a good price and not ask too many questions."

"So you just pick things up off the set?"

"Well, carefully, like. I mean, if you do it too obviously, people're going to notice, aren't they? I tend to do it sort of gradual." As he grew more confidential, the thickness of Tony Rees's Welsh accent increased.

"So you take something and hide it round the back of the set?"

"That's it. Then wait till it's quiet."

"Lunch break or some time like that?"

"Uh-huh. And slip it out at my leisure."

"I see."

"Oh, now come on," Tony Rees pleaded. "We needn't be talking about going to the police over something like that. I mean, that stiletto—I only got twenty quid for it. Hardly talking about the crown jewels, are we?"

"And the candlesticks?"

"Got a bit more for them, certainly. But, you know, I

reckon the company owes me a favor or two. I mean, all this rationalization and what-have-you they're doing . . . cutting down the overtime and the amount of jobs there are."

"So you reckon you've got to make it up somehow?"

"That's about the size of it, yes. Pick up what you can where you can."

"Do anything for money, you mean?"

"Why not? Don't look so bloody pious, Charles. Listen, commercial television's taking the public for a bit of a ride. I don't reckon it does any harm for them to be taken for a bit of a ride themselves. In a small way."

"You don't feel any guilt about stealing from them?"

"Course not. They don't notice it one way or the other."

It all sounded very plausible. Charles thought he probably had found the full extent of Tony Rees's criminal activity. But there were still details he wanted to check. "The candlesticks, Tony . . ."

"What about them?"

"When did you take them?"

"End of the last studio day that week. You know, the Thursday, because the Friday was canceled, wasn't it? There was such chaos in the studio at the end of that day, nobody knowing whether the set was going to stay up or be taken down, you could have walked away with anything."

"But that wasn't the first time you'd taken the candlesticks—or at least one of them—was it?"

The A.S.M. blushed.

"You took one on the Wednesday, didn't you?"

"Yes, but I put it back."

"Why? What actually happened?"

"Well, tell you what . . . Just after we broke for coffee, we'd done a scene of Stanislas Braid in his study. You know, sitting there and thinking, like—"

"I remember." It was the scene that had been frozen on the monitor when Charles had visited Rick Landor in the editing suite.

"Now, at the end of that scene, I was just clearing the set, and I noticed there's only one candlestick there."

Just as Charles had noticed on the monitor.

"So I thought, what the hell, some other bugger's nicked one. They'll have to get another pair, anyway. I may as well have that one."

"So you took it and hid it in your usual hiding place behind the set?"

"That's right."

"Then why did you put it back?"

"Well, bugger me if ten minutes later I don't go back on to that study set and suddenly notice that the missing one's been returned. I reckon they're more likely to look for one than two, so I pop mine back. Felt bloody relieved I did, too, actually, since the whole studio was swarming with police half an hour later."

"Yes." Charles nodded slowly. "And it was because you'd moved the candlesticks that you lied to the police about when you'd gone back into the studio . . . You know, later, when they questioned us at the rehearsal room?"

"Yes, well, don't want to draw attention to yourself, do you?"

"No." Charles was silent. Then he asked, "Tony, you

didn't see anyone either taking the first candlestick or putting it back, did you?''

"No, I didn't see anyone."

Someone had done it, though. Charles now had proof that someone other than Tony Rees had taken a candlestick during the break and replaced it shortly afterward.

He also felt fairly sure that while it was in his or her possession, someone had used the candlestick to kill Sippy Stokes.

Back at the hotel he was going to change his lager-stained trousers, but he met Will Parton and the others in the bar and, after a couple more large Bell's, went through with them to the restaurant. They were a large party and commandeered two tables, which they insisted the hotel staff put together. While they didn't actually behave badly, no one in the restaurant was left with any doubt that these were media people, who saw it as part of their mission to liven up Sunday night in Swanage—not, in the estimation of Will Parton, the most difficult thing in the world to do. "I've seen more get-up-and-go in a mortuary," he murmured at one point in the evening.

The group around the tables included Charles, Will, Rick Landor, Russell Bentley, Jimmy Sheet, Joanne Rhymer, and, surprisingly, Ben Docherty. The producer had said at the end of the previous week that he intended to stay in London, but either the need to see how his budget was being spent or the realization that he was missing a lot of W.E.T.-subsidized drinking made him change his mind, and he had driven down to Swanage on his own.

If it was the drinking that had drawn him, he was not destined to be disappointed. The "school treat" atmosphere of the jaunt encouraged them all to order a great deal of wine, and as they relaxed, their conversation became increasingly indiscreet.

"Here's to *Stanislas Braid*," said Will Parton, raising his glass, "the show that stands a chance now it's got rid of most of the dead wood!"

"What dead wood do you mean?" asked Charles.

"Oh, take your pick. W. T. Wintergreen? The bizarre Louisa? Sippy Stokes? Mind you"—Will leaned close to him for a moment and whispered—"there are a few other bits of pruning that wouldn't hurt."

"Like who, for instance?"

The writer looked across at the show's star. "Wouldn't do any harm to have Stanislas Braid played as Stanislas Braid rather than as Russell Bentley, would it?"

Charles grinned.

"How're the rest of the scripts going, Will?" asked Joanne Rhymer, who was sitting next to Charles (a state of affairs of which, incidentally, he heartily approved).

"All written months ago. But all no doubt to be *re*written right up to the moment of transmission." He smiled sweetly at his producer. "Isn't that right, Ben?"

Ben Docherty beamed benignly. He was at the stage of his alcoholic cycle when the drink mellowed him. "No, not a lot more. Nearly all done. Just those few tinkerings with the last episode."

"It shall be done, *Mein Führer*!" Will Parton barked with a cod Nazi salute. "I haff brought here ze book off ze famous Double-Vee Tee Vintergreen to achieve ze tinkerings zat vill be ze Final Solution of ze script."

Ben Docherty smiled paternally at his writer's excesses.

"Which book is the last one based on?" asked Charles.

"*The Transvestite Hermaphrodite Murder*," Will Parton replied, "in which Stanislas Braid is dragged kicking and screaming into the twentieth century."

"Ha. Ha. No, what is it really?"

"*The Medieval Crossbow Murder.*"

"Oh, well, I wonder which one of us will be killed by a crossbow bolt from the blue?" Charles mused aloud.

"Why do you say that?" asked Jimmy Sheet, suddenly alert.

Charles didn't actually know why he was embarking on this particular tack, but having started, he saw no reason not to continue.

"Well, think about it . . . We try to record *The Brass Candlestick Murder*, and we get stopped by an actual death."

"Not by a murder," said Jimmy Sheet firmly.

"We don't know that," said Charles, cavalier in his lack of caution.

"And certainly not a murder committed with a brass candlestick." Ben Docherty had now joined in the conversation.

"We don't know that either," Charles asserted. He was vaguely aware that he was being reckless, but his inhibitions were down, and he thought he might achieve some useful results by making his suspicions public. "I mean, suppose someone had decided they wanted to kill Sippy Stokes."

"I don't think this is in the best of taste," Rick Landor objected quietly.

No, it wasn't. Charles knew it wasn't. He was fully prepared to stop there, but Jimmy Sheet insisted, "Go on, Charles. This is interesting."

"Well, suppose someone decided to do away with the poor kid, took a brass candlestick off the set during the coffee break, lured her into the props room, hit her over the head with it, and then pushed the shelves of props on top of her."

After their recent rowdiness, the tables had gone very quiet. Charles knew he was a bit drunk and being rather stupid, but he had got to a point where he couldn't go back. His investigation into Sippy Stokes's death wasn't progressing. It needed a kick to get it moving again, and maybe what he was doing was providing that kick.

"You've been reading too many of the works of W. T. Wintergreen," said Ben Docherty flatly.

"Yeah, it's a load of cobblers, what you're saying," Jimmy Sheet agreed. "I mean, that could never have happened, anyway. And even if it had happened, it's the kind of thing you could never prove."

"You could prove it if there had been an eyewitness."

"But there wasn't no eyewitness," Jimmy Sheet persisted. "Which is just as well, because there wasn't anything for an eyewitness to see."

"How do you know?" asked Charles.

There was a new coldness in the former pop star's eyes as he enunciated, "Because Sippy Stokes died by an accident. And if anyone had witnessed an accident, they'd have bloody well come forward and told the police."

"They might not have done." Charles knew he was becoming irritatingly tenacious to his idea but reckoned an irritation factor might be useful in drawing reactions out of the assembled group.

"Are you saying," asked Ben Docherty, "that you witnessed Sippy Stokes being murdered?"

"No, I'm not saying that. I'm just saying that if she was murdered, then someone—not me but someone else— could have witnessed her being murdered."

"Any suggestions who?" asked Jimmy Sheet.

It was around then that Charles realized just how drunk he was. He also realized the insane risk that he was taking. If, as was possible, Sippy Stokes's murderer was sitting in that restaurant, then he was issuing a challenge. Almost, it could be said, issuing an invitation to the killer to see that Charles Paris was somehow prevented from making comparable suggestions again.

"No, none at all," he replied, caving in and trying to cover up his indiscretion. "No, I was only joking. Of course it was an accident, and of course no one saw it happen."

The conversation moved on smoothly to the prospects for the next day's filming, given the atrocious weather conditions. Charles felt foolish. He also felt uncomfortable and, for the rest of the meal, conscious that Jimmy Sheet, Rick Landor, and Ben Docherty were all looking at him with more than usual interest.

So, partly to dispel his unnerving awareness of their scrutiny, he went on drinking. And continued when the W.E.T. party moved into the bar at the end of the meal.

The rest of the evening passed in something of a haze. Charles remembered being, to his way of thinking, rather scintillating in conversation with Joanne Rhymer in the bar. He remembered how achingly like her mother she looked at close range.

He couldn't quite remember the sequence of words that

led to her telling him her room number and asking him to give her ten minutes. He could remember the excitement of anticipation and the unwise decision to have another drink to steel himself for the encounter ahead.

Then he remembered being awakened sometime later by Joanne and finding himself lying fully clothed on her bed. And he remembered all too well the dialogue that followed.

"I think you'd better be going back to your room, Charles."

"Yes. Yes, of course. Um . . . did anything happen?"

"No. No, nothing happened, Granddad."

And as the bed in his own room did aerobics beneath him, he remembered wondering whether Frances would consider that impotence made him technically innocent of the charge of making love to another woman.

And he remembered feeling fairly certain that she wouldn't see it that way.

And feeling that it wasn't a very good record, really. He'd promised Frances a year's abstinence from another woman. And—unless she'd excuse him on a doubtful technicality—he'd so far failed to achieve forty-eight hours.

CHAPTER
THIRTEEN

Corfe Castle is very properly a favorite spot for tourists. Apart from the castle itself—or rather its remains—which dominate the area from its hilltop setting, the village itself has a charm that has changed little from the beginning of the century. This obviously made it an ideal location for filming in the *Stanislas Braid* series. The cottages, built of fudgelike local stone and topped with slates of similar color, looked perfect with the Great Detective's vintage Lagonda drawn up in front of them. The sight of figures in thirties costumes pottering along the narrow streets struck no note of incongruity. True, double yellow lines had to be covered and shop fronts dressed up a bit, but the problems, compared to those presented by a London location, were minimal.

At last Rick Landor, as director, had the opportunity to

take a few long shots, confident that his perspective would not be marred by anachronisms.

Or at least he would have had the opportunity if the weather had not been so atrocious.

Though the visibility was slightly better than the evening before, rain still fell with a dispiriting evenness, and at times the cloud cover dropped low enough to obliterate the huge outline of the castle from the horizon. Cameramen and sound operators, wardrobe and makeup girls, cast and design staff, all clustered under bright umbrellas. The location caterers, whose van was stationed in a nearby car park, were kept busy producing bacon sandwiches to warm up sodden members of the production team. There were a lot of wet anoraks about.

And not just among the W.E.T. contingent. Even on a damp Monday morning in April a good few visitors had made the pilgrimage to Corfe Castle. Perhaps because the weather denied them the spectacular views they had hoped for or simply because they were mesmerized by anything to do with television, they seemed more than happy to regard the filming as a bonus tourist attraction. They clustered, unrecognizable and shapeless in anoraks of blue, yellow, and orange, behind the barrier that the location managers had erected, and followed the proceedings with great interest.

Charles Paris was not feeling at his best. He had been too preoccupied the previous evening to order a room-service continental breakfast and that morning had resisted the lavish spread offered in the hotel dining room. Anyway, all he really wanted was coffee, which he got from the caterers' van as soon as the brain-jolting coach trip from Swanage to Corfe Castle was over. He also, optimistically, asked for a bacon sandwich, but its salty smell and the greasy tentacles of fat creeping out of the bread made him shove it hastily into a litter bin before he threw up.

He felt wretched and awful, and his wretchedness and awfulness were compounded by the fact that he knew he had no one to blame but himself for feeling wretched and awful. Joanne Rhymer was on the set, but he kept clear of her, unwilling to confront that mock-innocent, sardonic smile.

What he really felt like was a hair of the dog. But he knew that was the way of disaster. He shouldn't. Better to punish himself by abstinence. Mind you, he couldn't erase from his mind the recollection that he had noticed an off-license just up the road.

The dreadful weather and the sepulchral light couldn't be allowed to stop the filming. Ben Docherty was footing the bill for a large number of people to spend two days on the Isle of Purbeck, and he was determined to get his money's worth, so Rick Landor started to galvanize his sodden team into action.

The setup of "The Seashore Murder" was that Stanislas Braid and his beloved daughter, Christina, together with Blodd, of course, were spending a few days' holiday in a quiet seaside town (whose calm was soon to be disturbed by a series of inexplicable murders along the seashore). The Braids had rented a small cottage in the seaside town (impersonated, needless to say, by the inland village of Corfe Castle), and by one of those coincidences beloved of W. T. Wintergreen, dear old Sergeant Clump was also taking his annual leave in a nearby boarding house, thus enabling him, even off his home patch of Little Breckington, to be appropriately baffled.

Charles had hoped the fact that the sergeant was on holiday might open out the possibilities of his wardrobe a bit, but no. One of W. T. Wintergreen's little jokes about the character was that his pride in his uniform meant that he took it off only to sleep (and in one of the books Stanislas Braid was even waggish enough to express his doubts over that).

The first scene to be filmed that morning was the detective's fairwell to his daughter outside their rented cottage. Three of the seashore murders had already taken place, and Stanislas Braid's intuition told him that he now had to go to Limehouse and consult what, with the insouciant anti-Semitism of the thirties, W. T. Wintergreen's original book had described as "a slimy Jewboy of a moneylender." (This had been cleaned up in Will Parton's script to "a rather dubious moneylender.")

The detective was therefore to be driven off to London by the faithful Blodd, leaving Christina to "enjoy the beauties of this wonderful summer, my dearest angel" (and, incidentally, to be put at risk of becoming the seashore murderer's fourth victim—a fate only averted by the timely return of Stanislas Braid with the solution to the crimes and an exciting clifftop rescue).

They rehearsed the scene in the disheartening mizzle. The film cameraman fiddled with his lenses and lights but eventually told Rick Landor there was no way he could make it look like a nice day.

"Will! Will!" the director shouted. "We're going to have to adjust the lines here."

"Why?" asked the writer belligerently as he emerged

from under an umbrella. He looked nearly as wrung out as Charles felt.

"We can't talk about 'enjoying the beauties of this wonderful summer' on a day like this, can we?"

"Don't see why not. It's no less realistic than everything else in the series." Will was evidently in a truculent mood.

"Oh, come on. You've got to think of something."

"Um . . ."

Russell Bentley got out of the Lagonda and scurried for the shelter of an umbrella. "God, what a shitty, piss-awful day," he muttered.

"Rick, how's about Stanislas tells Christina to 'enjoy the beauties of this shitty, piss-awful day'?" Will suggested innocently.

"Don't be bloody stupid!"

"Why not? In every other speech Stanislas Braid says what Russell feels like saying rather than what I wrote."

"Will, we're wasting time," Rick complained.

"Yes, come on, for Christ's sake!" said Ben Docherty, converting the bile of his hangover into professional anger. "We're slipping behind schedule. Think of a line for the bugger to say."

"Which bugger's this?" asked Russell Bentley, who Ben Docherty hadn't realized was in earshot.

"Er, um, Stanislas Braid," the producer replied hopefully.

"Oh, him." Russell Bentley was satisfied. The insult had nothing to do with Russell Bentley.

"How about"—Will Parton winced at the crassness of the cliché he was about to bring out—"'Enjoy yourself, Christina, my angel. Never mind the weather. Every cloud has a silver lining, and soon the sun will shine again for you, my precious one'?''

"Terrific," said Ben Docherty.

"Like it," said Rick Landor.

"Could you give me that exact text?" said the P.A., standing with pencil poised over her script. "What was it? 'Enjoy yourself, Christina, my...'?"

"I'm not sure." Russell Bentley decided it was time to make his contribution to the discussion. "I think there are a few too many of these 'my angels' and 'my precious ones.' I mean, she is his daughter, after all. It's not as if they were lovers."

"You never know," murmured Mort Verdon, as ever magically materializing when sexual innuendo entered the conversation. "Might be a smutty old cow, that W. T. Wintergreen. Maybe we should play up the soft-porn element in this series. Do wonders for the video sales."

"Anyway, we certainly don't want any hint of that," Russell Bentley continued. "I mean, I have a reputation in television, and let me tell you, any suggestion that I was involved in anything incestuous would—"

"There is no suggestion of that," Will Parton snapped. "It's just the way they talk. It's an idealized relationship. Honestly, in the period setting, nobody's going to think it sounds at all odd."

"I'm not so sure," Russell Bentley niggled on. "And I think it's something we should be very careful about. It's even worse in that scene we're scheduled to be doing tomorrow. You know, the one when I come back, the clifftop one. The affection between father and daughter in that does seem a bit over the top to me."

"Look, if you're finding the lines too difficult to play—" Will Parton began.

"Not a matter of that, dear boy." Russell Bentley as ever avoided using people's names. Which was just as well since he didn't know any of them. "I can play them fine, and dear, young"—he indicated Joanne Rhymer with a vague gesture—"is playing them fine, too. It's just, I think they're a bit too much."

"So what are you suggesting?" asked Will with withering irony. "That I should do a complete rewrite on tomorrow's scene?"

"Yes, that's it exactly," replied Russell Bentley, glad to have got his point across.

"I am not going to do any more bloody rewrites on this script!" shouted the writer.

"Well, I'm not going to do that scene tomorrow unless it's rewritten!" shouted the star.

Ben Docherty stepped between them. He was faced with a common producer's dilemma—a conflict of interest between the writer and the star. He had to take sides. But then he was a producer, so there was never any question about which side he would take.

"Actually, Will, I think Russell's got a point. Could you do us a rewrite on that scene by the end of today, please?"

The weather limited the amount of filming they could do in the village. Some lines could be adjusted to make reference to the rain, but scenes like the one in which Christina Braid was meant to set off from the cottage wearing a sun hat and carrying a deck chair just had to be postponed. The *Stanislas Braid* production team could only pray for better weather the next day.

Rick Landor did have one good time-saving idea, though. The script called for a lot of action on the cliffs overlooking the seashore where the murders had taken place. These were scheduled to be shot the following day on the nearby promontory of Durlston Head. But, given the misty conditions, Rick realized that some of them could be shot on the Corfe Castle hill. Over the far side of the ruins the land dropped away very steeply, and filming against that outline in a swirling mist would give a satisfactory illusion of the sea below. W.E.T. had already got permission to shoot a couple of other short scenes inside the National Trust property of the castle's grounds, so there would be no problem about doing a little extra. And it would save the time-consuming business of moving to another location that afternoon.

This was the kind of budget-saving thinking of which Ben Docherty heartily approved. As the director announced that they'd done all they could in the village that morning and they'd have an early lunch break before picking up again on the hill, the producer went across to congratulate Rick on his prudent housekeeping.

Charles could put it off no longer. He went to the off-license to buy a half bottle of Bell's. But once it was safely installed in his raincoat pocket, he decided that his fragile condition required something less ferocious than whiskey. A pint of bitter would be more gentle therapy; that'd sort him out.

Walking across to the pub, Charles saw Tony Rees chatting to some of the anorak-shrouded tourists who had been watching the morning's activities. The A.S.M.

moved away as he saw Charles approach and called out to the crowd, "No more excitement here today, I'm afraid. Fun's over. We'll be filming up at the castle this afternoon, but you'll have to pay your entrance fee to see that."

The tourists walked quickly away, and Tony gave Charles a slightly anxious grin. "Not still thinking of going to the police, are you?"

Charles shook his head, an unwise thing to do to a head in its condition.

Two pints later there seemed to be a possibility of life continuing. As often happened, the beer had rediluted the residue of the previous night's alcohol, and he felt drunker than two pints should justify. Still, he did also feel better. It really was dreadful how another drink always made him feel better.

And he was suddenly ravenously hungry. He hurried across to the car park and loaded a plate up with sausages, eggs, and chips from the location caterers' van. Then, rather than having his lunch diluted by the rain, he took it into one of the coaches. A sheepish look around as he got in confirmed, to his relief, that Joanne Rhymer wasn't there. He sat in a vacant seat next to Mort Verdon.

"How're things, boofle?"

"Better for a drink."

The stage manager nodded. "Rumor has it you were up to the old bed-hopping again last night."

"Untrustworthy source of information, rumor."

"Oh, yes." They were silent for a moment. "Nice, was it?"

"Not one of my greatest triumphs."

"Dear, oh, dear." Mort Verdon shook his head in pity. "Perhaps you'd do better with a man, you know."

"Who can say?" said Charles. "Trouble is, I'm afraid it's never appealed that much."

"Ah, well . . . Don't know what you're missing, boofle."

"So I'm told."

At that moment Tony Rees's face appeared over the top of the seat in front. "Mort, have you got the schedule for the next episode?"

"Yes, it's in my little duffel bag. Front of the coach."

"Do you mind if I have a look at it? Something I want to check."

"Be my guest."

The A.S.M. moved down to the front of the coach.

Mort Verdon's eyes narrowed. "Wonder what he's up to?"

"Why should he be up to anything?" asked Charles innocently.

"Because he always is, that's why."

"What kind of things?"

"Fiddles, little deals, anything that gives his W.E.T. salary a bit of a lift."

"Helping himself to props and what-have-you?"

"Well, let's just say if Corfe Castle is found mysteriously to have gone missing at the end of this afternoon's filming, I think we'll know in whose knicker drawer to start looking for it."

The solidity of what remains of Corfe Castle after the demolition efforts of parliamentarian sappers and explosives in 1646 is a testament to the strength of its medieval structure, but the castle is only a skeleton of what it once was. Parts of the old keep stand upright, a landmark above the town, but around them there is a rubble of toppled towers and broken masonry. It has the air of a folly built by a crazed aristocrat, an ideal setting for some tale of Gothic horror.

This quality was enhanced that April afternoon by the drizzling mist that kept lifting and descending over the castle's remains. Rick Landor and his cameraman did their best but kept having to break off when the visibility would suddenly drop to about ten meters. At such times there seemed a real danger of losing members of the *Stanislas Braid* team. Figures loomed eerily out of the mist, and it was impossible to see until they came close whether they were actors, production staff, or the few sodden tourists who resolutely continued sight-seeing, even when there were no sights to see.

But slow progress was made in the filming. When the clouds lifted, the outline at the edge of the hill looked very convincingly like a cliff above an unseen sea, and at those moments Rick Landor and Ben Docherty urged their cast into action, fearful of wasting a second of the precious light.

The scenes were fortunately short ones, without too much dialogue. Stanislas Braid, Blodd, and Sergeant Clump were tracing the footsteps of the murderer, looking for the clues that would once and for all convict him and send him to the gallows. Sergeant Clump would point to footprints that the Great Detective instantly identified as being weeks old; only Stanislas Braid himself was allowed to find "the mark of a size seven-and-a-half riding boot that has been recently repaired by an apprentice cobbler and whose scuffed heel tells us that its wearer is afflicted by a slight deformity of the right leg . . . probably the legacy of a childhood attack of rickets.''

Slowly, as the afternoon progressed, one by one these scenes were immortalized on film, but the weather was deteriorating fast. The clouds seemed to descend more frequently, and each time they lifted, the cameraman winced more when he checked his light meter. Eventually, at about a quarter to four, he shook his head firmly and said, ''No point in doing any more. The quality just won't be good enough.''

''Oh, I'm sure it will,'' cajoled Ben Docherty, as ever more concerned about his program's budget than its quality.

''No way.''

''Well, look, let's not call it a 'wrap' yet,'' the producer pleaded. ''Keep everything set up, give people a twenty-minute tea break, and then see if the light's improved after that?''

The cameraman shrugged. ''All right, you can if you like. But it's a waste of time. The light won't get any better today.''

''Can't we put more artificial light on it?''

''I'm using all the lights I've got.''

''Oh, well, look, let's take the break, anyway, and see. What do you say, Rick?''

''Okay. You're the producer, Ben,'' said the director in a way that left no doubt that he was in complete agreement with his cameraman.

The tea break was announced. Russell Bentley complained that there wasn't time to get back down to the car park and the caterers' van, so Mort Verdon was unwillingly dispatched down the castle hill to fetch up thermoses of coffee and tea. The production team dispersed, wandering off into the mist—some, like the few remaining tourists, to indulge in a little abortive sight-seeing, others to check whether there were any parts of the castle where Cromwell's army had left enough roof to provide a little shelter from the constant soft but saturating rain.

Charles Paris was feeling bad again. Under the weather, he thought to himself with a grim little smile. The lift given by the lunchtime beer had worn off, and his headache was back with temple-stretching ferocity. With it, the headache brought remorse, the knowledge of how deeply he had humiliated himself the night before. And how thoroughly he had betrayed his intentions toward Frances.

He knew he had no alternative now. The half bottle of Bell's from the off-license still thumped reassuringly against his thigh in the pocket of the raincoat he had put on over Sergeant Clump's damp blue uniform. A quick slurp might pick him up again. Just the one. Really. Then a quick bite to eat when they got back to the hotel. Nothing to drink and a very early night.

What else could he do to make himself feel virtuous? Ring Frances? But no, he decided on consideration. The memory of the previous evening was too raw for him to risk speaking to his wife. In his current abject state he'd probably confess everything. And that was hardly going to advance the cause of their *rapprochement*, was it?

He didn't want anyone on the production team to see him drinking. It wasn't that he was a secret drinker, he told himself—the circumstances were exceptional. He just needed this one drink to get him through the rest of the day's filming. (He conveniently forgot that there was unlikely to be any more filming that day.) Then, after that one drink, no more. Nothing that evening. Maybe have a few days on the wagon. No booze at all for a while. Good idea, yes.

He walked away through the remains of the keep, along the ruins of the new bulwark and down toward the southwest gatehouse. Around the corner of that, at the foot of the old bastion, he would be sufficiently out of sight to have his quick medicinal drink. (Guilt made his planning so elaborate; given the heavy mist, he could in fact have nipped around the corner of any outcrop of masonry and felt pretty confident of being unobserved.)

As he sloshed through the long, wet grass at the foot of the keep, he thought he heard something. Hard to tell through the deadening mist where it came from or exactly what the sound was. A cry, perhaps an animal's cry, and a heavy thump.

He thought nothing of it as he moved forward. He took the half bottle out of his pocket and heard the reassuring click as he broke the seal on its golden top. He raised the bottle to his lips and was about to take a long, restorative swallow when he saw an indistinct shape on the ground ahead of him.

He walked toward it, feeling suddenly cold.

The shape had a human form. But it looked foreshortened, the head unnaturally folded under the body.

He recognized the clothes but turned the dead weight over to confirm his worst fears.

It was Tony Rees. Still warm. He had only just landed. The thump Charles had heard had been the impact that had so immediately and thoroughly broken the A.S.M.'s neck.

The mist suddenly swirled and lifted, and Charles could see up to the window in the broken wall of the keep some thirty feet above him.

No one was visible in the dark frame of the window. But a few minutes earlier, Charles felt certain, someone had been there.

The person who had pushed Tony Rees to his death.

Who was also, Charles would have risked a substantial bet, the person who had murdered Sippy Stokes.

CHAPTER
FOURTEEN

"Of course it was murder," said Charles, looking moodily out of the window of Will Parton's room at the foggy darkness of Swanage Bay.

"You have no reason for saying that," the writer argued. "In those conditions, with the wind and the fog and the stones all slippery, anyone could have lost their balance and fallen off that windowsill."

"Yes, but why would anyone *be* on that windowsill in the first place? Tony'd have had to climb all the way up there. Why would he do that—unless he had arranged to meet someone?"

"I've no idea, Charles. It seems to me that playing Sergeant Clump is going to your head. You're seeing murders everywhere."

"Doesn't it have that effect on you—working on the series? Don't you start to see murders everywhere?"

"No. All I start seeing everywhere is *more bloody rewrites!* Like this one." Will Parton gestured at the screen of his lap-top computer. "Just because Russell Bloody Bentley doesn't want his screen image tarnished by a whiff of incest. Personally I think that'd do it a lot of good—first interesting characteristic he's shown in his entire film or television career."

There was a silence. Will Parton tapped away at his keyboard.

"You don't suppose Russell could have killed him, do you, Will?"

"Oh, for Christ's sake, Charles, shut up! I can't imagine Russell killing anyone . . . or doing anything else that requires any exercise of the imagination, come to that. And what possible motive could Russell have had for killing Tony Rees?"

"I don't know. Blackmail, maybe? Tony was into everything . . . anything he could use to screw a bit of money out of people. I wouldn't be surprised if he was into blackmail. If Russell had some dark secret—"

"Russell's only dark secret is that he's as thick as two short planks. And it's not much of a secret; it's self-evident to everyone who meets him."

"I do like this blackmail idea, though. Maybe not Russell. Jimmy Sheet, perhaps? He's scared witless his wife's going to find out about his dalliances with other women."

"He doesn't appear to have any dalliances with other women at the moment."

"No, but it seems he did with Sippy Stokes."

"Certainly looked that way, yes." Will Parton stared at Charles in sudden alarm. "Oh, my God! Sergeant Clump doesn't think that Sippy Stokes was murdered, too, does he?"

"Yes, I do."

"Charles, why do you have to get into all this? Why pretend you're as good as Stanislas Braid? Why not be content to remain as Sergeant Clump and be baffled?"

"I have good reasons for thinking Sippy Stokes was murdered."

"Do you? Well, I have good reasons for wanting to get this bloody rewrite finished. The main one being that as soon as I have finished it, I am going down to the bar to treat myself to a very large drink. Look, why don't you just go down there, get yourself one in, and wait for me? If I can get a run at this *without interruptions*, I'll be through in about twenty minutes."

"No, I've decided I'm not going to drink anything this evening."

"Oh, Goody Two Shoes. Afraid of getting into more inappropriate beds, are you?"

Charles blushed. Will Parton grinned and returned to his keyboard.

"Of course," Charles mused after a time, "Tony Rees might have had something on Rick Landor."

Will Parton slammed his fist down on the table. "Charles, will you please shut up!"

"No, but listen, I've had a thought. Suppose Tony Rees actually witnessed the murder of Sippy Stokes."

"Assuming that such an event ever took place."

"And then he tried to blackmail the person who had done the murder?"

Will Parton yawned.

"Which was why he got killed."

"Yes, well, thank you," said Will in the tone of someone ending a conversation. "I don't promise anything, but I'll see if I can get that into ep. five as a subplot."

"Oh, my God!" said Charles suddenly.

"What the hell is it now?"

"I've just thought— You remember how I was behaving last night?"

"Hard to ignore it, I'm afraid, old man. Hard for Joanne to ignore it, either, I would imagine."

Charles ignored the gibe. "You know, I was talking at dinner about Sippy Stokes possibly having been murdered."

"Yes."

"And I did sort of imply that someone might have witnessed the killing."

"Hmm."

"You don't suppose the murderer then got suspicious of Tony Rees and that's why Tony got murdered?" The enormity of the idea that Charles might have inadvertently caused someone's death turned him cold.

"No, I don't, Charles," said Will in the last stages of exasperation. "All I suppose is that if you don't shut up, there'll be another murder. *You* will be the victim, and *I* will be the perpetrator. Got that?"

"Yes. Sorry."

"Now will you please leave me alone to finish this bloody script! You've got your own room, haven't you?"

"Yes."

"Well, go to it. Give me twenty minutes; then we'll go and have a drink."

"But I—"

"You can have Perrier."

"Well, I—"

"Go to your own room, sit down, read a good book. Or failing that"—Will picked up an old hardback from the table and flung it across to Charles—"read *this*."

It was a copy of *The Seashore Murder* by W. T. Wintergreen.

"Thanks very much," said Charles without enthusiasm.

His lack of enthusiasm proved justified. W. T. Wintergreen may have seen Frances through her romantic teens, but she wasn't really Charles's sort of writer. He found the style distinctly arch, or perhaps "twee" was a better word?

But the extracts he read considerably raised his estimation of Will Parton's technique. The adaptations had filleted their originals with great skill, stylizing the old-fashioned elements in a way that made them much more acceptable to modern tastes.

He could also understand Russell Bentley's objections better from the book than he could from the scripts. Once again Will had done a good job in diluting the W. T. Wintergreen text. In the book the Stanislas Braid/Christina Braid relationship was nauseatingly sugary.

He threw *The Seashore Murder* down onto his bed—it had only taken ten minutes for him to get bored with it—and focused his mind on Tony Rees's death.

The blackmail idea did appeal. It conformed with what he knew of the A.S.M.'s character, and it also provided an obvious link between the two deaths.

If Tony had witnessed Sippy Stokes's murder and then started to blackmail its perpetrator, that would provide a perfect reason for him to be silenced.

But it needn't have been the murder. Tony Rees might have known another secret about someone involved in *Stanislas Braid*. Who could say what indiscretions the various suspects might have committed in their pasts?

There was of course one person who probably *could* say. Charles shuffled through the back of an old out-of-date diary from which he had never bothered to transfer his address list, found a London number, and dialed it.

"Hello?"

"Maurice, it's me, Charles."

"What on earth are you ringing me at home for? There's nothing in this business so urgent that it won't wait till the morning."

"It's not about business."

"Oh? What is it, then?" Maurice sounded suspicious.

"I want some information."

"What kind of information?"

"A bit of show-biz gossip."

"Dirt?" Maurice's tone had changed. Now he sounded very alert, almost enthusiastic.

"Dirt," Charles confirmed.

"Dirt on who?"

"There are four people I'd like you to check out."

"And what sort of stuff do you want?"

"Oh, any indiscretions in their past. Criminal . . . or personal. . . . The sort of stuff they'd want kept quiet, anyway."

"I get you."

"Do you think you can do it?"

"Charles," his agent said reproachfully, "need you ask?"

"No, of course not. Sorry."

"Right," said Maurice Skellern gleefully. "Give me the names."

With that line of inquiry launched, Charles once again brought his mind to bear on Tony Rees. He tried to recall everything he had seen the A.S.M. do over the previous twenty-four hours and think if there was anything that struck a discordant note.

The first strangeness was the young man's unexpected affability in the pub the night before. After nearly a fortnight of avoiding Charles, suddenly Tony was grasping him by the arm and buying him drinks. There must have been some explanation for the change.

The other thing that hadn't seemed odd at the time but might, in posthumous retrospect, appear slightly strange was Tony's request that lunchtime for Mort Verdon's production schedule. Why should the A.S.M. suddenly want to know what was happening in the next episode when they were in the middle of filming on this one?

Of course, there were any number of innocent answers to that question, but Charles thought it just might be worth checking out. He reached for the phone again and dialed the number of a room in the hotel.

"Hello?" The voice was not suspicious but guarded.

"Mort, it's Charles Paris."

"Oh, hello." The voice opened out. "Seen the error of your ways at last, have you, boofle? Thought you would. Well, just give me a moment to slip into something casual and then"—the stage manager dropped into a Mae West impersonation—"come up and see me."

"Ah, sorry to disappoint you."

"Story of my life, boofle," said Mort, and dropped

instantly out of their customary masquerade. "What *can* I do for you, then, Charles?"

"It's about schedules."

"Hang on a moment while I just control my excitement. *Schedules*, did you say?"

"Yes."

"*Production* schedules?" asked Mort, as if the world could hold no topic more exciting.

"Yup."

Mort's voice subsided into flatness. "What about them?"

"You remember that Tony—the late Tony—borrowed your schedule for the next episode at lunchtime today?"

"I do remember."

"Did he give it back to you?"

"No. No, he didn't. But, quite honestly, I'm not going to hold it against him. I mean, the poor boy's dead, and I'm hardly going to go and get stroppy with his next of kin and demand my schedule back at a moment like this, am I? Mind you, I can't think the details of the next episode's filming and studio are going to be much use to poor Tony where he's gone."

"No," said Charles. "It's strange . . ."

"What?"

"Well, you know I found his body."

"Yes. I'm sorry. Seem to be making rather a habit of that at the moment, don't you?"

"Mm. Mort, I shouldn't have done this, but before I went to get help, I checked through Tony's pockets."

"Macabre thing to do."

"Yes, I suppose it was a bit. Anyway, your schedule wasn't there."

"Oh, well, as I say, I'm not about to make a great fuss."

"No. I also looked through Tony's bag on the coach . . . You know, before the police came to take it away."

"Quite the little Sergeant Clump, aren't we?" murmured Mort, echoing Will's words.

"Yes. Thing is, your schedule wasn't in his bag either."

"Well, Charles, boofle, I don't think we have to alert Interpol straightaway, do we? It is, after all, only a few photocopied sheets we're talking about. Tony might have dropped it, he might have shoved it in a litter bin, could be anywhere. Don't worry, I'll get another one before we start rehearsing that episode."

"Yes, yes, fine. Well, thanks, Mort."

"No problem. And don't forget, Charles, if you wake up in the night feeling a little queer, you've got my room number."

"Thanks. I'll bear it in mind."

Charles put the phone down and looked out pensively into the murk beyond the windowpane.

The telephone trilled, and he picked it up again.

"It's Will. I've finished the sodding thing. Let's have that drink. Pick me up on the way."

"Come in. It's on the latch."

Charles obeyed Will's instructions and went into his room. The writer was scribbling a note on a blank sheet of paper. His portable printer was rattling out the rewritten scene. It stopped. With practiced ease, Will Parton tore off the perforated strips on the sheets and shuffled them neatly into order.

"This one's for Russell, since he's the one who, in theory, has to learn the stuff. I'll do copies for Ben and Rick later. I'm parched."

With satisfaction he put the note on top of the pile of sheets.

"DEAR RUSSELL," Charles read, "HERE'S THE REWRITE. YOU CAN'T COMPLAIN NOW. ALL CLEANED UP. NO ONE COULD IMAGINE IN THEIR WILDEST FANTASIES THAT THERE WAS ANYTHING OUT OF THE ORDINARY IN THE RELATION-SHIP BETWEEN STANISLAS BRAID AND CHRISTINA. YOURS, WILL."

"Are you going to give it to him now?"

"No," said Will. "I'll drop it into his room later. Don't want to get involved in discussions about how the part of Russell Bentley should be played at this precise moment. My first priority is a drink. Come on." At the door he asked, "And you're certain you're not going to be drinking tonight?"

"Certain," said Charles.

They stayed in the bar most of the evening. Charles survived one round on Perrier, but then he reasoned that he really did need a large Bell's. That afternoon a sudden death had once again stopped him when he was about to have a drink. And he was in a serious state of shock after finding Tony Rees's body.

There was only one interruption in his evening's drink-ing. After they had been in the bar for about an hour, he was paged by Reception. There was a telephone call for him.

It was Maurice. Calling back with the dirt. Charles

spent ten minutes in the phone booth by Reception scribbling furiously in a notebook. All interesting stuff. Then he went back to continue drinking.

"Really must get that script to Russell," said Will at the end of the evening as they tottered toward his room.

He fumbled with the key, but as he leaned against the door, it gave and opened inward. "Stupid twit. Must have forgotten to lock it."

They stumbled into the room. Will looked at the empty table with an expression of puzzlement.

"That's funny," he said. "Someone's taken my rewrite."

CHAPTER
FIFTEEN

The next morning the weather seemed little improved, so there was no chance of picking up the summery scenes in Corfe Castle. But since the precedent of a misty seascape had already been established the previous afternoon, the decision was made to shoot as much of the seashore stuff as possible on Durlston Head. The W.E.T. coaches therefore drove through Swanage and up out of the town to the location. Tony Rees's death had put a damper on everyone's spirits; there was no sign of the hilarity of previous coach trips.

The location caterers were already set up in the car park when the coaches arrived, and many of the crew, who had only half an hour before finished large hotel breakfasts, immediately tucked into their first bacon sandwiches of the day.

By this time the weather did look rather more promising. Every now and then the clouds parted to admit a few frames of watery sunshine. The cameraman began to look as optimistic as the lugubrious traditions of his trade allowed.

Ben Docherty urged Rick Landor on to get the morning's filming finished as quickly as possible. If they could have all the Durlston Head stuff in the can before lunch and if the weather continued its promising trend, there would be a reasonable chance of getting the outstanding Corfe Castle scenes done in the afternoon. In spite of deaths and climatic disasters, the producer was still determined to get his series made in time. The thought of having to spend another day in Dorset was too awful to contemplate. The next day's rest day was obligatory by union rules, so if that got moved on, all the studio bookings would have to be shifted. The cumulative effects over the series didn't bear thinking of. Even overrunning on that day's schedule offered the direful prospect of overtime payments. The producer tried, unsuccessfully, to disguise his panic as efficiency.

The disappearing rewrite of the night before had not been explained, but fortunately the text was on the memory of Will's lap-top, and he had been just sober enough to get it to print up other copies. Everyone seemed happy with the changes. Russell Bentley, in particular, was effusive in his praise of the writer's efforts. He still couldn't remember Will's name, but he did enthuse, "You've done frightfully well, old boy. Must get you writing something else for me."

The scene that had caused all the fuss was a tense little moment of drama in which Stanislas Braid and Christina appeared to be trapped on a clifftop ledge with no hope of escape. In the W. T. Wintergreen version they took this as an opportunity to tell the depth of their feelings for each other. Will Parton's rewrite had changed it to something altogether more jokey. The affection was still there, but masked in a kind of flippant bravado.

The new scene, however, was not scheduled for shooting till later in the morning. First, a few laborious moments of Sergeant Clump and Blodd had to be filmed as they wandered in panic along the cliff path, looking for the missing detective and his daughter. These scenes were very short—Blodd rushing into shot and saying something like "No sign of them," then rushing out of shot, to be followed seconds later by a ponderously puffing Sergeant Clump—but there were long pauses between them as Rick Landor and the cameraman tried to find new vantage points and angles along the cliff path.

In one of these breaks Charles took the opportunity of checking Jimmy Sheet's reaction to the death of Tony Rees. "Dreadful business yesterday, wasn't it?"

"What's that, then?" asked the former pop star.

"Tony."

"Oh, yeah." Jimmy Sheet grinned unpleasantly. "Don't think anyone'll miss him."

"No, I gather he had his less pleasant qualities," Charles prompted.

"Huh. You can say that again. Nasty bit of work. No secret was safe when you got someone like that around."

"Oh?"

"Still, he isn't around, so that's no longer a problem, is it?"

"Did you find it a problem?"

Jimmy Sheet gave Charles a hard look. "What's that to you?"

"Just wondered."

"Well, I'd advise you to stop wondering. Tony Rees is dead, and from my point of view that's the best thing that could have happened to him."

"How do you think it did happen?"

Jimmy Sheet looked Charles straight in the eyes with insolent self-assurance. "He fell, didn't he?"

They got the searching of the cliff path filmed, and Charles's scenes were finished. Needless to say, Sergeant Clump was not bright enough actually to find the missing detective. No, as ever, he was baffled. It was Stanislas Braid's own ingenuity that got him out of this particular fix. As it did out of every other fix in which he found himself.

But although his work was done, Charles had no alternative but to stay around the location. No transport would be going back into Swanage until the Durlston Head scenes were finished, and he didn't fancy walking five miles.

So he sat on one of the stone benches thoughtfully placed for sightseers to look out over Durlston Bay. The weather was continuing to improve and, although leaden clouds hung like a Roman blind over the horizon, he could get some impression of the beauties of the Isle of Purbeck's coastline.

He looked up to see Ben Docherty approaching. The

producer sat down beside him and said with a nervous grin, "All done?"

Charles nodded. He reached into his raincoat pocket and pulled out the half bottle of Bell's. Though its seal had been broken, the contents were still intact. "Fancy a drop?"

"Wouldn't say no," said Ben. "Bit nippy."

Charles wondered how he could broach the subject of Tony Rees's death but was saved the trouble, because Ben Docherty did it for him. "That business yesterday, Charles . . ."

"What?"

"The A.S.M."

"Oh, yes."

"You found him, didn't you?"

"Uh-huh."

"I mean, you *found* him? He was there when you got there? You didn't see him fall?"

"No, I didn't."

The answer seemed to please Ben Docherty, who nodded slowly. "The police talked to you?"

"Yes."

"You didn't gather from them what they thought had happened?"

"Police never give much away, do they?"

"No, no," the producer agreed slowly. But his mind was still not at rest. "And there's no talk round the cast?" he asked diffidently.

"Talk about what?"

"Well, about Tony's death."

"Obviously everyone's *talking* about it, but"—time

for a bit of tactical obtuseness—"I'm sorry, I don't quite understand what you mean."

"I just mean, Charles, nobody's sort of suggesting, you know, like maybe the death wasn't an accident?"

"I haven't heard anyone say that," said Charles. Which was true enough. Present company, of course, excepted.

"Good," said Ben Docherty. "Good."

Thermoses of coffee were brought from the caterers' van. "Can we make it a short break?" Rick Landor pleaded. "Just ten minutes. We're doing well, but we've still got a lot to do."

Charles, feeling rather dozy after his whiskey with Ben Docherty, accepted a cup of coffee. Rick also had one, which he downed in three nervous gulps. "Getting there, getting there," the director said.

"And the studio stuff's relatively straightforward this week, isn't it?" asked Charles.

"Not too bad. Should be simpler than the last one I did, anyway."

"What do you mean?"

"Come on, Charles, you remember what it was like. I'm glad I wasn't the one to have to do the dirty deed, but it's a great relief to have had W. T. Wintergreen banned from the premises. She didn't make that week easy for me."

"And then, of course," said Charles casually, "there was Sippy Stokes."

"Yes, yes, there was." The director was silent for a moment. "Sounds dreadful to say it, but I'm afraid this episode'll be a lot easier without her around."

"Oh, but I thought she was your casting."

"Yes, I suppose she was. I mean, I put through the booking, but I was under pressure."

"Who from?"

"Sippy herself. Doesn't do to speak ill of the dead, but I'm afraid she was a nasty bit of work."

"Weren't you lovers, though?"

"Yes, we were. But I'd tried to break it off many times. She wouldn't let me. The trouble was, she knew things about me which—well, things that could have got me into quite a bit of bother."

Yes, thought Charles, remembering the information that Maurice had supplied him with the night before. Something to do with your cocaine habit, perhaps?

But he said nothing as Rick Landor continued, "Anyway, giving Sippy the part of Christina was a kind of once-and-for-all payoff."

"She blackmailed you into casting her?"

"That's what it amounted to, yes. It was a habit she had, one of her less endearing habits."

"Hmm. Do you think she tried the same trick with Jimmy Sheet? You know, threatened to tell his wife after they'd been out together?"

"Let's say it wouldn't have been out of character if she had."

"I see."

They gazed out over the sea. It was almost blue. The dark clouds were moving away to the west. It looked as though they would get all the Corfe Castle summer scenes safely done that afternoon.

"Bad luck, really," said Charles, "having two black-mailers in the same production."

"What do you mean?"

"It was a bit of a sideline for Tony Rees, too, I gather."

Rick Landor abruptly looked at his watch. "Got to get on," he mumbled. "Check out the eyelines we've got on the next setup." And he moved away.

Charles stayed looking out over the sea. He didn't seem to have progressed far in his search for the killer of Sippy Stokes. Or the killer of Tony Rees, come to that. He felt certain that the two deaths were linked, almost certain that the same person had perpetrated both.

Jimmy Sheet . . . Ben Docherty . . . Rick Landor . . . Each one of them had a secret to hide. A secret Tony Rees might easily have found out about. Each one of them was a potential suspect.

And of course there was one other potential suspect involved in that morning's filming on Durlston Head.

He found Russell Bentley sitting in a folding chair, a white towel tucked biblike around his neck, while a makeup girl tried to make him look like a man who has just fallen off a cliff and clawed his way back up to it to find his beloved daughter stranded on a ledge.

The makeup girl's job was not an easy one. While Russell wanted to look authentically battered, he didn't want any marks on him that might be deemed disfiguring. A discreet scratch along the temple was fine, so was a bruise on the cheekbone, but he wouldn't tolerate anything that spoiled the shape of his nose or the outline of his jaw.

The makeup girl did her best to meet these exacting conditions. She had the tools of her trade on a little tray propped up on a stand beside her. Bottles and cakes of various flesh tones. Liner pencils. Spirit gum. Brushes and sponges. A bottle of Arterial Blood to authenticate the scratches. She did not look up from her task as Charles approached.

"Russell..." he began.

The star squinted up into the sun. "Oh, hello, er..." Once again the name escaped him.

"Pity about Tony Rees, wasn't it?"

"Who?" But the star knew; Charles could see it in his eyes. Russell Bentley was just using his notorious amnesia for names to play for time.

"You know. The one who died up at the castle yesterday."

"Oh, yes. Tragic business." The sentiment was automatic; there was no hint of real emotion in his voice.

"I suppose so," said Charles. "It seems he was a nasty piece of work, though."

"Really? I didn't know him at all."

"Apparently he was the kind of person who would find out secrets about people, secrets they very definitely wanted kept quiet, and then he would make the people pay for his silence."

"Would he? I don't really see what this has to do with me."

"No." Charles allowed a few seconds' silence. "You got your way over the rewrite, then?"

"Sorry?"

"The scene with Christina. The one you're about to film."

"Yes. Well, it does make the whole relationship much more relaxed. And less emotionally charged. I mean, they are father and daughter, after all."

"Yes, and you have your reputation in television to consider."

"Exactly."

"Wouldn't do for the public to think Russell Bentley was the kind of man to be involved in incest."

"No." The star held up a cautionary hand to the makeup girl, who was poised with her brush and bottle of Arterial Blood at the ready. "Not too much of that stuff. Don't want to look like Rocky IV."

"Or," Charles persisted, "the kind of man to be involved with underage girls."

A new light came into Russell Bentley's eyes. "What are you talking about?"

"Some parties back in the early sixties. Involving people working on a film called *The Hawk's Prey*."

From the expression on Russell Bentley's face Charles knew that, as ever, Maurice Skellern's information had been correct.

"I don't know what you're talking about," the star lied, trying to bluster his way out.

"Oh, I think you do. And I think Tony Rees also knew what I was talking about."

"Nonsense. I'm certainly not going to—"

But the star never said what he was certainly not going to do. There was the sound of a gunshot from somewhere behind Charles. He saw the shock on Russell Bentley's face at the sight of the red stain spreading over the towel that covered his throat; there was more expression there at the moment than the star had ever shown in his portrayal of Stanislas Braid.

As Russell Bentley slumped back in his chair and the makeup girl screamed, Charles turned and started up the hillside toward the clump of trees where the gunshot had come from. Brambles snatched at the blue serge of Sergeant Clump's uniform; branches of shrubs slashed at him as he thundered forward. He pushed aside the branches of a tree and suddenly stopped dead.

In front of him stood someone with a bewildered look and a gun.

It was W. T. Wintergreen.

CHAPTER
SIXTEEN

She looked at him for a moment, her face still puzzled. Neither of them spoke.

Then, suddenly, she fled.

She showed a surprising turn of speed for a septuagenarian, and given Charles's surprise and the fact that he was out of breath from his dash up the hillside, she had twenty meters' start on him before he got his legs moving.

He pulled after her and might have caught up to her over a longer distance, but W. T. Wintergreen had not far to go. She burst out of the clump of trees from which the shot had been fired and raced across the hillocks of long grass to a rough track, where her old black Beetle was parked.

The driver's door was open. She leaped in and slammed it. By the time Charles was close enough to do anything, the engine had sputtered into life. He just had time to catch a glimpse of the tear-stained face of Louisa Railton in the passenger seat as the car screeched away, sounding like a demented lawn mower.

He stood still, sweating and breathless, as the Beetle diminished into the distance.

Then, attempting to reorganize in his mind everything he had ever thought about the murders, he moved slowly back down the hill.

Russell Bentley was not dead. When Charles came to think of it, he couldn't imagine Russell Bentley ever dying—just going on being Russell Bentley for all eternity.

He wasn't even injured. Nor, though she was in a state of hysterics, was the makeup girl. The bullet fired from the hillside had missed both of them. By remarkable good fortune, though certainly aimed at Russell Bentley, what it had hit had been the bottle of Arterial Blood in the makeup girl's hand. The ghastly stain on the star's towel was courtesy of Leichner rather than of his own arteries.

In fact, except for the makeup girl's hysterics, the incident had had little effect on the *Stanislas Braid* production team. Russell Bentley was of the opinion that it hadn't been a gunshot, anyway; he thought the bottle of Arterial Blood must have been flawed and have broken spontaneously. The makeup girl swore she had heard something, but she was in too emotional a state for anyone to take what she said very seriously.

And Charles Paris, the one person who knew that a

shot had been fired, for reasons of his own kept that
knowledge to himself.

The filming continued, and the Durlston Head scenes
were finished before lunch, much to the delight of Ben
Docherty. The weather had cleared completely, and there
was every prospect of getting the Corfe Castle scenes
shot within the time allotted. His precious budget looked
as if it had survived another threat.

Charles Paris went in the W.E.T. coach back to the
hotel in Swanage. There was no point in his returning to
Corfe Castle, and he told Mort Verdon that he would
make his own way back to London.

He packed quickly and at the hotel Reception organized a cab to take him to Bournemouth. From there he
caught a train to Waterloo.

And all the time he was on the train, Charles Paris sat
and thought.

When he arrived in London, he knew what he had to
do, but he felt he needed some bolstering before he did
it. Not his customary alcoholic bolstering, though; the
situation was far too serious for that. No, he needed
human contact. He needed to tell someone what he was
about to do.

What he really needed was to talk to Frances. He even
got as far as standing in a phone box in Waterloo Station
and lifting the receiver.

But he chickened out. Frances would be at school. She
could be extremely frosty and headmistressy when he
rang her at school. Anyway, the memory of Sunday
night's shame was still with him. No, he should wait to

ring Frances until he felt cleansed and virtuous, until he felt worthy of ringing her. He had a nasty sense that that feeling could be a long time coming. Reluctantly, he put the phone down.

Then he looked at the departures board for the next train to Richmond.

No killing time before this visit. He asked the taxi driver to take him straight to the cottage and watched as the cab drove away.

The black Beetle was parked outside. He knocked on the door, and it was opened by W. T. Wintergreen.

She looked strained, and her eyes were pinkish from recent tears. But she carried herself with a kind of calm dignity.

"Ah," she said, "I had expected you might come." She stood back to let him into the tiny sitting room. "Can I offer you a cup of tea or coffee, perhaps?"

There was something incongruous, given the circumstances, about these genteel observances. Charles refused the offer of refreshment with matching gentility.

He sat edgily on the chair his hostess had indicated. Reading his mood, she said, "You don't need to feel any anxiety, Mr. Paris. It's all over now."

He sensed that she was telling the truth and relaxed partially.

"So I suppose it's just confession time," said W. T. Wintergreen with a sigh.

"I suppose it is."

She nodded slowly. "It is my intention to make a full confession to the police. However, Mr. Paris, I am quite happy to run through the details for you if you so wish."

"I would be most grateful," he said, amazed at how easily he was dropping into her own, slightly formal, style of speech.

"Yes. You see, I have not been unaware of your interest in this little . . . series of murders."

"Oh?"

"And I congratulate you on finding out as much as you have. As someone who has spent much of her life bending her mind round the problems of detective fiction, I can recognize a brain which works in a similar fashion."

"Oh, thank you." Charles really appreciated such a professional compliment, but once again he couldn't help being struck by the incongruity of this conversational square dance.

"I suppose," said W. T. Wintergreen in a manner that was almost languorous, "it is the fiction that is to blame for everything that has happened. I don't mean because it was crime fiction that I wrote. That is irrelevant. What you have been investigating have not been the actions of an unhinged old lady who can no longer distinguish fictional crime from real crime. No . . ."

She was silent. The faded eyes were unfocused behind their spectacles.

But she pulled herself together before Charles had to prompt her. "No, I suppose you might say that I have been protecting my creations."

"Stanislas Braid? Christina? Sergeant Clump?"

She nodded slowly. "Yes, yes, that is exactly it. When you were last here, Mr. Paris, I remember our discussing the creative process, discussing how involved writers become with their characters."

"How much of themselves they put into those characters," Charles suggested gently.

"As an actor, of course you would understand. Well, most writers can cope with the problem. They get deeply involved with their characters while they're writing the books, but then they... have a break, go on holiday, they... get back to normal. I suppose it depends really on how much else they have in their lives. In my case, there hasn't been much else in my life."

"Looking after your father till he died?"

"Yes."

"Not, I gather, the easiest of men."

"No, not the easiest. Very jealous and— He was jealous of my writing. He was the reason why I stopped writing."

"So, as your own life became more circumscribed, more claustrophobic—looking after your father, looking after your sister—you retreated more and more into the world you had created in your fiction."

"Yes." She let out a brittle little laugh. "I gather the American enthusiasts of the crime-fiction genre have now designated a special category of the 'cozy' British mystery. And I suppose it is a 'cozy' world. Everything looked after, everything tied up. All emotions neatly cut off at the ends, not fraying and tangling like real emotions. And a sense of justice, the knowledge that Right will triumph, reinforced, of course, in the days when I was writing, by the existence of the Death Penalty. At the end of the book the criminal would be unmasked, and the reader could sleep easy in the confidence that the murderer was meeting his Final Retribution."

"And then, of course, there was the character of Stanislas Braid himself, wasn't there, Winifred?"

"I cannot deny that he had a certain appeal for me."

"A lot easier to deal with than most of the real men you had encountered."

W. T. Wintergreen allowed herself a little smile. "More containable, certainly."

"A lot easier to deal with than your father?"

Her mood changed abruptly. "These murders," she said, "this series of murders. I expect you have gathered most of what happened, but I'll spell it out for you.

"First," she continued briskly, "that dreadful actress. I'm afraid I had been in a very emotional state ever since the idea of the television series was mooted. It had been a long time since I wrote the last Stanislas Braid book, and all this new interest brought back a lot of things I thought I had forgotten. I was unhappy with many of the ideas that the television company proposed. The actors and actresses did not look as I had visualized the characters, though I may say you, Mr. Paris," she conceded, "were not physically inappropriate for the part of Sergeant Clump."

"Oh, thank you," said Charles.

"But the girl . . . the girl who was meant to be Christina . . . In all the books her fair hair and blue eyes are described. Suddenly for me to see this . . . swarthy Mediterranean type . . . was a profound shock. And she was so far from the *soul* of the character."

Charles had wondered how long it would take before souls came up again.

"Actually killing her," said W. T. Wintergreen, "was an impulse, hardly a decision. That morning, at the end of the break, I saw her walking out of the studio. I was near the study set. I took the candlestick, hit her with it in that little room, pulled the shelves down on top of her, and returned the murder weapon. The whole sequence of events took . . . less than a minute, I would think. Afterward I could hardly believe it had happened, it was all over so quickly.''

Charles looked thoughtful. ''For someone who has devoted so much of her life to devising devious and ingenious methods of killing people, your own first attempt at murder was a bit amateur.''

''I agree. As I say, it wasn't a rational choice, just the impulse of a moment of insanity.''

''Yes.''

''But it seemed to achieve the right effect. The dreadful girl was gone, and suddenly the new Christina is everything she should be. She looks right, and she has this wonderful ethereal quality of childish innocence.''

Charles cleared his throat, recollecting the real character of Joanne Rhymer.

''So I did not feel guilty about the murder. It seemed to have been right. Everyone seemed happier. And though I was slightly shocked that I could have been capable of something like that, I was able to put it from my mind.''

''You had no intention at that stage of committing further murders?''

''Good heavens, no.''

''So what did Tony Rees do to make you change your mind?''

''Ah.'' She was silent for a moment. ''Well, you may recall that during the recording of the second episode there was an unfortunate exhibition in the studio?''

"When Ben Docherty banned you from the premises."

"Yes. Extremely regrettable. And for me devastating. Because, although much of what was happening to *Stanislas Braid* caused me deep disquiet, I was obsessed by the series. I still felt a need to watch everything that happened, every rehearsal, every piece of filming. I felt it was . . . my baby."

She used this phrase as if she had just coined it and nobody in the history of the world had ever used it before. A tear glistened in her eye. She reached up under her glasses and brushed it clumsily away before going on. "I was devastated by the prospect of being excluded from my own series, so I had to find some way to keep in touch."

"And Tony Rees saw you out of the studio," Charles suddenly recalled.

"Exactly. When we reached the Reception of W.E.T. House, I asked him whether, for a financial considera-tion, he would keep us in touch with the production schedule."

"You chose the right person. For a financial considera-tion Tony Rees would have done anything."

"He certainly didn't need too much persuading. But at least we now had a way of keeping vaguely in touch with what was going on. Of course, we were not allowed in the studios, but they couldn't keep us away from the filming."

"So you and Louisa were down at Swanage from the start?"

W. T. Wintergreen nodded, and in Charles's mind a whole new set of ideas tumbled into place. "In fact, you were in that pub I went into on the Sunday evening. You were sitting in the alcove with Tony—you had your backs to the door—and he only came up to me in such a friendly way because he didn't want me to see you."

"Yes."

"And the reason he spilled his drink over me was only to distract my attention while you two went out of the pub."

"That is what happened, yes."

"I've just realized something else," Charles continued in a burst of excitement. "You and Louisa were in the crowd, all wrapped up in anoraks, when we were filming in Corfe Castle. And that was why Tony Rees wanted to borrow Mort Verdon's schedule for the next episode. He gave it to you up at the castle that afternoon."

A nod confirmed this.

"So why did he have to be killed?" asked Charles quietly.

"He said he had actually witnessed the murder of Sippy Stokes."

"I see." Charles was pleased to have another of his conjectures proved right. "And he wanted a large price for his silence?"

"A much larger price than I could afford to pay."

"So you pushed him out of the window in the castle ruins?"

"It was not intentional murder. Again, I wasn't thinking straight. I was angry. There was a scuffle. He fell. I didn't know at the time that he had died."

"Convenient that he had, though."

"Oh, yes. Very convenient."

"Which brings us," said Charles, "to Russell Bentley."

"Russell Bentley . . ." W. T. Wintergreen looked drained;

the emotional strain of her confession was beginning to tell.

"Let me say what I think happened, Winifred. You tell me if I'm right."

She nodded acquiescence.

"It wasn't what he was doing to the Stanislas Braid character that worried you so much as what he was doing to the Stanislas/Christina relationship. His constant desire to play down the emotion between the two of them upset you. That relationship was for you one of the most important parts of the books, and he was trying to kill it. Then, during the filming in Corfe Castle, you heard Russell arguing that one of your favorite scenes, the avowal of Stanislas and Christina's love for each other when their lives were threatened, should be rewritten. You found the rewrite in Will Parton's room, with the note on it saying that it was all Russell's idea, and from that moment Russell Bentley was your next target. Am I right?"

"You are right," she conceded graciously. "And so this morning I hid myself near where you were filming, and when my opportunity came, I shot him. My third murder."

"No," said Charles.

"No?"

"You missed. Russell Bentley isn't dead."

W. T. Wintergreen slumped with a little sigh against her chair. "Thank God."

There was a long silence in the tiny sitting room. Finally, Charles asked, "Where's Louisa?"

"Upstairs," W. T. Wintergreen replied softly. "Upstairs. I

will be going to prison. I will not be able to look after her anymore. Louisa needs someone to look after her."

"Yes." Charles smiled grimly. "Can I see her, Winifred?"

The bedroom was on a scale with the rest of the cottage. It was decorated in the subtlest of pastel shades. The wallpaper was almost white, with a tiny motif of a pale yellow flower. Under an eiderdown of the palest pink, her head propped up on a pillow of the same color, lay Louisa Railton.

Her hair was neatly brushed and laid out across the pillow. Her eyes were closed, and her body was completely relaxed. There was no movement.

Charles looked across at the old crime writer. Down Winifred Railton's lined cheeks tears flowed unchecked.

"There," she said, "Mr. Paris. The last in my series of murders."

CHAPTER
<u>SEVENTEEN</u>

"No," said Charles Paris. "It's the first."

"What do you mean?"

"I mean that you have never murdered anyone outside your fiction. Until today. And this"—he indicated the body on the bed—"I think would qualify as a mercy killing rather than a murder."

"I did kill them," W. T. Wintergreen asserted. "I did."

Charles shook his head.

"Why don't you believe me, Mr. Paris?"

"I don't believe you partly because of your personality. You say you committed the murders in fits of irrationality, but you aren't the sort of person to suffer from fits of irrationality. Your head is far too firmly screwed on for you to behave as you claim to have done. Yes, the Stanislas Braid books are very close to your heart. And yes, you were upset by some of the things W.E.T. was doing to your property, but you wouldn't have committed murder—not for something like that.''

"You don't know. You don't know me that well," she objected defiantly.

"Another giveaway," Charles went on, "was your reaction just now when I told you Russell Bentley hadn't been hurt this morning. If you were the crazed, irrational creature you claim to be, you would have been disappointed because the latest in your series of murders had failed. But no, you were relieved, deeply relieved that another life had not been wantonly lost."

There was a silence. Then she announced firmly, "I'm going to the police, and I'm going to tell them exactly what I've told you."

"Yes, I'm sure you are," said Charles. "And maybe they'll believe you, and maybe they won't. I should think, if someone like me can see through your story, professional police investigators wouldn't have much difficulty in doing the same."

"But I—"

"The reason you're going to the police is because the police have been in touch with you, isn't it?"

She nodded. "The police in Dorset talked to us yesterday after Tony Rees's death. Then, in the evening, we had a call from Scotland Yard, the people who have been investigating the actress's death. They said they wanted to talk to us. Either we could fix a time, or if we hadn't made contact within twenty-four hours, they would come and find us."

Charles looked at his watch. "And your twenty-four hours is nearly up."

"Yes."

"Which is why you killed Louisa."

"As I said, she couldn't cope with my being away." W. T. Wintergreen frowned, as if in pain. "I don't like you talking about my killing her. She didn't feel a thing. I often put her to bed with her sleeping draft, but this time I just gave her a larger dose. She's all right now. She won't have to know about any of this, any of the unpleasantness."

"You've always protected her from unpleasantness, haven't you?"

"She was never very strong. She found life . . . difficult."

"So do most of us. But very few are lucky enough to have someone like you to keep the world at bay."

He moved across to Louisa Railton's girlish dressing table and picked up a silver-framed photograph. The picture showed a beautiful girl in her early teens. But for the anachronism of the haircut and the collar of the dress that showed at her neck, it could have been Joanne Rhymer. "I can see why you were so pleased when the part was recast." He turned to face W. T. Wintergreen. "Louisa was Christina, wasn't she?"

"I don't know what you mean."

"Oh, I think you do. I think you wrote the books partly for her."

"Well, perhaps partly. We were very close." The old bespectacled eyes strayed across to the bed, as if hoping that its occupant would suddenly come back to life.

"As you said, the books were 'cozy.' They dressed up unpalatable things in a palatable form. Murder, the ultimate crime, is dressed up as an intellectual game. And other crimes—equally offensive crimes—were also dressed up and sanitized.''

''I don't understand what you're talking about, Mr. Paris.''

''Yes, you do. Stanislas Braid was your father, Miss Railton.''

''No, he wasn't. As I said, our father was a very difficult man, and Stanislas is—''

''I mean that Stanislas Braid was how you dressed up your father. Just as you dressed up your sister as Christina. And the idealized relationship between the two of them was how you dressed up the rather less attractive reality of the relationship between your father and your sister.''

She let out a little gasp, staggered slightly, and found her way to a bedside chair.

''I'm right, aren't I?'' murmured Charles.

Very slowly, the old head nodded. ''In those days such things weren't talked about. You didn't have them blazoned across every newspaper and television program. But yes, after our mother died, our father did''—she swallowed—''start to touch Louisa.''

''And she never really recovered from the trauma?''

''No, I suppose not. I don't fully understand these things, but certainly...in some ways my sister never grew up. She couldn't cope with life.''

''So it went on for some years?''

''For some years, yes. In a way, I don't think Louisa realized there was anything wrong. She loved him, you see, and she thought love made everything all right. So long as he was alive, she was strange, maybe immature, not fully grown-up, but it was after he died that she really broke down.''

"And from then on you had a full-time job looking after her. Which is why you never had time to start writing again." W. T. Wintergreen acknowledged the truth of this with an almost imperceptible nod. "And was it after your father's death that Louisa started to become obsessed by the Stanislas Braid books?"

"Yes. She'd always liked them, been amused by them, but after our father died . . . yes, she became obsessed by them."

"So she was the one whose whole identity was threatened by the changes that W.E.T. was making to the books, particularly changes to the character of Christina or Christina's relationship with her father."

W. T. Wintergreen made only a token gesture of dissent at this.

"I think, Miss Railton, that almost everything you told me downstairs about how the murders were committed was true, so long as you cast Louisa in the role for which you cast yourself. She was the one who saw Sippy Stokes in the studio and was seized by the impulse to pick up that candlestick."

"She—my sister was not well. She had times when she was not herself."

"Yes, and you nursed her through all of them. But she had never committed murder before, had she?"

W. T. Wintergreen shook her head.

"And then she told you what she'd done. Told you, I would imagine, with pride. And that news put you in such an emotional state that you weren't up to going into the studio the following day.

"But you managed to put it from your mind. The death seemed to be accepted as an accident, the new

Christina was wonderful, the chances for success of the series seemed greatly improved. As you said, you could almost believe that the crime hadn't happened.''

"Yes."

"Until the murder of Tony Rees. With that one I don't think what you said downstairs was quite accurate. When you claimed that you had killed him, you said it was an accident. But Louisa murdered him quite deliberately, didn't she?"

There was no response.

"And when I saw you on Durlston Head this morning the reason you looked so bewildered was not because you had just shot at Russell Bentley but because you had just snatched the gun from Louisa after she had shot at him."

The old lady was silent. She no longer made any attempt to deny the truth of what he said.

The silence in the childlike bedroom extended for a long minute. Then, with an effort, W. T. Wintergreen clamped her hands on to the arms of the chair and heaved herself wearily upright. "Well, I think I'd better get to see the police now. Don't want to put them to the trouble of coming out to fetch me."

"And when you do see them," Charles Paris asked, "will you tell them the truth? Or will you continue to do what you've spent all your life doing and protect your sister?"

"That," W. T. Wintergreen replied with dignity, "is my decision." And with something that was almost a grin, she continued: "The one inalienable right of crime writers in their own stories is to choose whodunit."

CHAPTER
__EIGHTEEN__

Outside, for the first time that year, June had decided to blaze, but no dribble of sunlight percolated through the grimy windows of the St. John Chrysostom Mission for Vagrants Lesser Hall. The only effect of the change in the weather had been to reheat the trapped, moted air inside to a new staleness.

It was the first day of rehearsal for the last episode of *Stanislas Braid*, "The Mashie Niblick Murder." There had been much discussion about this title. Though that was what the original W. T. Wintergreen book had been called, Ben Docherty had been of the opinion—with some justification—that the average member of the I.T.V. audience hadn't a clue what a mashie niblick was. Will Parton, taking a perverse liking to the title, had argued that golf was a very popular television sport. The producer had countered that though golf was indeed popular, clubs were now referred to by numbers and not by exotic names.

"We must definitely change the title," he had said firmly.

"No, we mustn't," Will Parton had said equally firmly. "The original book was called *The Mashie Niblick Murder.*"

"Oh, come on," Ben Docherty had objected. "You've changed everything else. Why this sudden conscience about the title?"

The argument had gone back and forth for some time, until the producer pulled rank and said he was in charge of the series, he would make that kind of decision. And his irrevocable decision was that the title should be changed.

This conversation, however, had taken place in the morning. Later in the day, when Ben Docherty, the alcohol dying in him, was at the nadir of his midafternoon listlessness, Will Parton had simply handed his typescript over to the P.A. with instructions for her to type it up as it was, title and all. By the time the producer noticed what had happened, "The Mashie Niblick Murder" had appeared on too many forms and schedules for it to be worth the effort of alteration.

With the progress of the series, listlessness had become Ben Docherty's dominant mood, and from him the rot seeped through to everyone else involved in the production. The gradual realization came that as a television series *Stanislas Braid* was actually not very good. W. T. Wintergreen's books were dull and dated, and in spite of Will Parton's valiant efforts, the scripts never quite escaped being dull and dated, too. A charismatic central performance might perhaps have lifted the whole venture, but as the series went on, Russell Bentley's limitations became increasingly apparent. He was basically a very wooden actor.

No one ever actually said the series was going to be a disaster. Indeed, to use the word *disaster* would have been overstating the case. The programs would go out, and be dutifully watched with half an eye in those millions of households where the control was never moved from I.T.V., but they would never rise above the gently slopping surface of customary television mediocrity.

In the early days of the production much had been said about prime placings, about the series "spearheading the autumn schedules," but gradually such talk died away, to be replaced by rumors of *Stanislas Braid* being "held over," even rumblings of that worst of all fates, "being held over till next summer." The summer schedules, everyone knew, were the Sahara of television, in which programs slowly dehydrated and perished, unseen and unmourned.

In the same way, the talk of a second series, which had been rife during the first month of recording, trickled away to nothing. The second-series options on the artistes, so carefully agreed by their agents and the W.E.T. casting directors, were destined never to be taken up.

No one commented on these changes. They had all been in the business long enough to have experienced plenty of previous dashed hopes. The only positive reaction came from Jimmy Sheet. Finally realizing the true quality of the vehicle in which he had been intended to make his mark as an actor and remembering who had recommended it to him, he sacked his agent. Then, deciding that he still hadn't wrung all there was to be wrung out of the music business, he started organizing a final international concert tour. He also made a killing on property deals in Miami and started buying up office blocks in Rio de Janeiro.

Other less organized members of the *Stanislas Braid* production team also started to make plans for what to do at the end of their contracts.

Russell Bentley was already committed to a national tour of a venerable stage thriller, which a new producer was convinced could follow the path of other venerable stage thrillers through the provinces and into the West End. So the star, who had by now lost interest in his performance as Stanislas Braid, was much exercised in going through the playscript, deciding which lines would have to be changed before he could fully realize his customary performance as Russell Bentley.

Joanne Rhymer, by diligently working her way through all of the straight men involved in *Stanislas Braid*, had by the end of the series achieved full Blue Nun status. This was confirmed by the arbiter of such distinctions, Mort Verdon. She was, needless to say, going straight on to another job. Ben Docherty had introduced her to a London Weekend Television producer, who, impressed by the range of Joanne's talents, had booked her instantly for the role of the hero's girlfriend (and who knew what else) in his forthcoming series.

Her mother—surprisingly, given the usual duration of her liaisons—was still with Ben Docherty. As soon as recording on *Stanislas Braid* was completed, the producer was going to take Gwen Rhymer on a gastronomic tour of France. Assuming he survived the alcoholic and physical demands of that, he would then return to W.E.T. to supervise the remaining postproduction work on *Stanislas*

Braid and to start work on "an exciting new project." The exciting new project was a drama series about adolescent problems for schools. Though this assignment might be seen by outsiders as a demotion from the mainstream of television drama, Ben Docherty's boss had assured him that it was "a key appointment in a pivotal area." What this meant was that the commercial television franchises were shortly going to be up for renewal, and W.E.T. was making one of its periodic assertions of concern in the area of public-service program-making.

Rick Landor, having directed the penultimate episode of *Stanislas Braid*, had some editing and sound dubbing to do on the series and then would be moving on to direct a game show for Thames Television. His ambition of a feature film remained as far off as ever.

Will Parton's ambition was a major serious stage play. He had had the idea for years; it was just a matter of finding the time to write it; and throughout the series he had been promising himself that he would settle down to the play, ignoring all other distractions, the minute his work on *Stanislas Braid* was finished.

But then he had had an offer from Yorkshire Television to script a series they were doing about nineteenth-century medical pioneers. Only take about three months ... Well, four or five months with the rewrites. And the money was, once again, very good. Will spent a whole evening with Charles Paris in the W.E.T. bar, agonizing over his dilemma, before making the inevitable decision. After all, he reasoned, it was only five months maximum. And the extra money would give him even more of a cushion when he got down to writing what he really should be writing. So the major serious stage play, a project of which he was growing increasingly terrified, was deferred yet again.

Charles Paris himself had, needless to say, not made any plans for what to do when his W.E.T. contract expired. Presumably, the following week would see him once again signing up at Lisson Grove Unemployment Office, just around the corner from W.E.T. House. It was ironic, really. While he was working there, he had no need to take advantage of that accident of geography, but the minute his employment ceased, he would have to start making the trek over again.

He'd feel the draft a bit when he was back to just the giro check. He had had no difficulty in accustoming himself to the regular W.E.T. money. Or in spending it with equal regularity. Come the end of the final recording in less than a fortnight's time, it would all be gone. And, of course, on such earnings there would be tax to pay. . . . Still, that was next year's problem.

He looked around the St. John Chrysostom Mission for Vagrants Lesser Hall and thought how thoroughly W. T. Wintergreen had been forgotten. No one in the rehearsal room, except for Charles Paris, was aware of her own small crime and her sister Louisa's greater crimes. No one was aware that she had made a confession to the police and been arrested. Nor that in prison, awaiting a trial that must surely have released her, she had quietly died, her life perhaps without purpose after her sister's death.

Charles Paris had been the only person from *Stanislas Braid* to attend the quiet cremation. Had it been one of the actors on the series who had died or a member of the production team, W.E.T. would have been effusive in representation and flowers, but then no one really knew about W. T. Wintergreen's death. And, after all, she had been only a writer.

The scene in the rehearsal room was predictable. As foretold by Maurice Skellern, read-throughs had been abandoned, and rehearsals now began straightaway, with blocking movements around the taped-out sets on the floor. Russell Bentley was arguing over some line that he felt was out of character. Ben Docherty was saying it might need changing. Will Parton was remonstrating violently that he wasn't going to do any more bloody rewrites. Joanne Rhymer was coolly eyeing the young actor who was that episode's murder victim.

In other words, it was business as usual on *Stanislas Braid*. Charles Paris's eyelids were heavy. Maybe he could doze off a little of the previous night's excess before they got to the first Little Breckington Police Station scene.

Must start looking around for some work, he thought lazily as he drifted off. Not a good time of year, though. Very quiet, the beginning of the summer, as Maurice Skellern always said. Mind you, Maurice Skellern always said every other time of year was very quiet, too.

There was something else, though, wasn't there? Something else niggled in Charles's mind. Something he'd been intending to do for six weeks or so. What was it?

Oh, yes. Of course. It was Charles Paris's last thought as sleep took over: Must ring Frances.

SIMON BRETT is the author of thirteen Charles Paris mysteries as well as a collection of short stories and four other novels. A scriptwriter and radio and television producer, he is a former president of the British Crime Writers' Association. He lives in England.